book two of the silver sequence

SILVER CITY

cliff mcnish

Carolrhoda Books, Inc. / Minneapolis

First American edition published in 2006 by Carolrhoda Books, Inc.
Published by arrangement with Orion Children's Books, a division of Orion Publishing
Group Ltd., London, England

Carolrhoda Books, Inc.
A division of Lerner Publishing Group
241 First Avenue North
Minneapolis, MN 55401 U.S.A.

Website address: www.lernerbooks.com

Library of Congress Cataloging-in-Publication Data

McNish, Cliff.
    Silver city / by Cliff McNish.—1st American ed.
        p. cm.
    Summary: The children drawn to Coldharbour prepare to battle a terrifying force
headed their way.
    ISBN-13: 978-1-57505-926-6 (lib. bdg. : alk. paper)
    ISBN-10: 1-57505-926-6 (lib. bdg. : alk. paper)
    [1. Fantasy.] I. Title.
PZ7.M478797Sil 2006
[Fic]—dc22   2005020618

Manufactured in the United States of America
1 2 3 4 5 6 – BP – 11 10 09 08 07 06

For my grandmother, Bertha McNish

contents

the unearthers

THOMAS

Night, and I stood watching all the children in the world leaving their homes. For a moment the drone of an overhead surveillance plane drowned out their voices; then the plane passed by and their eager conversations and rushing footsteps could be heard again.

All those feet, running. Most children couldn't help themselves. Whatever place they came from, if they had any energy left they always ran the last stretch into Coldharbour. My time to be summoned had come earlier, but I'd been just like these other children. Not even thinking to leave a note for my parents, I'd left home and come breathlessly rushing into this place.

From a side street outside Coldharbour, I saw a teenage girl accidentally clatter into a boy.

"Sorry," she said, steadying his arm. "Are you okay?" She pointed towards the silver light ahead. "Look, we're nearly there!"

"I know," he said, grinning. "How do you feel?"

"Happy," the girl said. "Nervous, as well. A bit anyway."

"Me, too." He laughed. "But we got here, didn't we? We made it."

"Yes. We did." The girl took his hand, and together they sprinted down the final sloping streets leading the way into Coldharbour.

Coldharbour. Until yesterday it had been little more than a seven-mile expanse of mud and rubbish dumps bordering the sea. Apart from myself and five other special children, the only things living there had been seagulls and a good supply of well-fed rats. The only people who ever disturbed the rats were a scattering of bored gang kids with nothing better to do.

Not anymore. As I gazed out over the mud, I couldn't begin to count the numbers of new children settling inside Coldharbour.

They'd been arriving all night. For hours I'd watched them running here, leaving everything they knew behind. Most weren't even properly dressed. They turned up in socks, slippers, pajamas, vests, nightgowns, T-shirts, or whatever else they'd been wearing when they received the call. Some teenagers had waited long enough to throw on coats or decent footwear before leaving home, but not many.

Attempts were being made to stop them, of course. No doubt some quick-acting parents managed to haul their own kids back indoors if they caught them in time. And as the night dragged on police units also arrived, taking up positions all around the area. In western Coldharbour army brigades had even driven in, hurriedly erecting barricades to prevent anyone from crossing the roads over the river. The barricades didn't work. Children fought their way past. Naturally a few got caught, but most escaped and were soon trying to get inside again.

I knew what was happening. I knew because I'd been just the same as these other children. A few weeks earlier, I'd been determined to get here. I'd even hid on the way, hid from my own Mum and Dad, to make sure they wouldn't force me back home.

But, if anything, these new children seemed even more resourceful than I'd been. To get within Coldharbour they were prepared to do anything: argue, lie, join together, create a distraction—whatever they had to. It was a kind of madness, because there was nothing for us in this place: no home, no food, no shelter.

So why were we all here?

Because Milo drew us. That's all we knew. Yesterday evening, shortly after sunset, a child with a body over four miles long and with wings five times that size had appeared in the sky over Coldharbour. A vast silver-glowing child, spanning towns and the sea.

And the moment he appeared, children couldn't help themselves: they were drawn to him. It wasn't a question of choice. There was no choice; they had to reach him.

Just after dawn the next morning, with the sun peeking over Coldharbour's eastern rubbish dumps, I stood watching a skinny little boy push through the perimeter crowds. He stumbled past me, lifting his arms skyward to be picked up. "Milo! Milo!" he called out plaintively over and over, the way all the youngsters did. "Mil-o!"

I followed the skinny boy's gaze upward. And there he was, floating at cloud level, and gleaming in the sky—Milo, the silver child.

His body-shape was like any other boy's, but that's where any resemblance to us ended. His wings left you breathless. I'd watched children walking under them for hours without reaching their end. Those colossal wings! At first I'd thought they were made of feathers, but when you judged the weight of the body they were holding up, you realized the wings couldn't possibly be made of feathers. Something better than that. Something finer. Stronger and more enduring.

With occasional flexes of the wing tips, Milo kept himself stationary. He remained in one fixed location of the sky, dead center over Coldharbour. His body lay flat and parallel to the horizon, his bare feet swaying ever so slightly, his face sometimes tilted towards us, sometimes towards the sky.

Protecting us. That's what we all felt, anyway.

For now, at least, it was only the weather Milo protected us from. Gazing out to sea, I could see it was raining heavily, but in Coldharbour we didn't feel a drop.

Milo's body arched over us like a shield. There wasn't even much wind. With gentle ripples of his wing-edges, Milo held the cooler breezes at bay; he kept us warm.

I turned away from the sea, continuing my tramp around the northeast limits of Coldharbour. A vast assortment of children and families were making their way towards the entrances, but the adults who'd managed to follow their children this far were in for a shock. They were about to discover the Barrier. The Barrier was an invisible line surrounding Coldharbour. It marked the last point at which adults could accompany their children inside. We passed through the Barrier freely; parents were held out. It wasn't a hard physical obstacle, something that could be smashed down. The Barrier only responded to flesh. It somehow knew the age of flesh. It let children and animals in and kept all adults out.

None of us had any idea why.

I leaned against a wall for a while, witnessing the awful parting of parents and children along the Barrier's edge. Not far away, the skinny boy I'd spotted earlier was still shouting his head off at the sky. There didn't seem to be anyone looking after him. "You on your own?" I asked. "No brothers or sisters?" The boy blinked, and I tried again. "Who did you come in with, then?" He continued to blink at me, smiling politely but not understanding a single word I said. A foreigner, maybe. I decided to try out my language skills on him. "*Mama?*" I ventured. "*Papa? Da? Mor?*" I was running out of foreign words.

The boy looked vaguely East European to me. I didn't know any East European words. I knew a German one, though: *Mutti*. I tried it. The boy stared at me as if I was an idiot.

A youngster alone like this wasn't a common sight. On the way to Coldharbour, the majority of single kids had joined up with others like themselves. The child-families, they were already being called: huge new families composed entirely of unrelated children. By the time they reached us many had been traveling together for so many hours that they'd become good friends.

The boy I'd come across must have got detached from his group somehow. Luckily another noisy crowd was just behind me. It was a big child-family, dozens of mixed boys and girls. Squashed into the confines of one of the final streets leading into Coldharbour, they marched at a brisk pace, singing nonstop. French songs, I think. Maybe from an exchange school somewhere along on the coast.

"*Bonjour!* This one's on his own," I called out. "Can you take him?" I don't think the kids at the front understood, but a girl beside them did. She swept up my boy and hoisted him onto her shoulders. Then the whole lot of them headed on confidently down the hill, making an incredible racket with their singing. The skinny boy loved it. He had a great view, and the last I ever saw of him he was piping out his own version of the song, getting every word wrong.

Milo's head—that huge hairless domelike skull of his—was directly above me. I looked up at him, and he appeared to be looking right back. It was an illusion—his eyes were so enormous that you couldn't help believing he was watching you all the time. Milo kept his left eye eternally pointing down towards us. His right eye was more flexible than ours, and was positioned on top of his head. He kept it facing upwards, towards the heavens. Towards the stars.

We all knew what Milo was looking for there.

The Roar.

A few weeks earlier I'd been one of just six children in the world who could hear the sound of the creature we called the Roar. Helen, a mind reader, was the only one of us with any idea what the Roar was. She'd tried to describe it to me. A brutal creature, she'd called it. A beast more immense than our world. And famished.

A vast starving creature hunting us from the stars.

We original six children—Helen, me, the twins, the giant boy Walter, plus Milo himself—were the beginning of a defense against the Roar. We were, as Milo said, the first generation of children; we led the way. Milo had actually still been a normal boy when I first met him a few days earlier, though he'd already lost the use of his arms. When we found each other, he was in such pain. The changes needed to turn him into the defender to come were only part finished. Using my unique gift, I helped complete them.

That unique gift was what the twins called *beauty*. It was a talent to find out whatever a child needed most— and then give it. A way into a child, Emily described it once. A way to warm it up, or console it. Or, in Milo's case, to lessen the pain of his transformation. That's what Milo had required from me. My beauty had given him the strength to endure long enough to become the silver child above us.

Milo was the forerunner, the first of the great defenders. His duty was to protect us all. To help him do so, he called the rest of the world's children to him, gathering them into a single location so that could he shield them from the Roar.

The Roar. That distant terrifying voice. Once Milo appeared in the sky all the world's children could hear it. There wasn't a single one of us left who hadn't at some point in the last few hours been brought to tears by the sound of it. Sometimes the screams the Roar made were like a knife, stopping you cold; other times they were barely loud enough to register, but even those smaller shrieks cut through everything else.

We understood almost nothing about the Roar. There was, however, one truth all of us understood. I don't know how we knew, but none of us had any doubt: the Roar intended to feed on us.

As soon as it was close enough, the feeding would begin.

Not wanting to think about that, I huddled closer into

my jacket and carried on walking. It had been several hours since I'd said good-bye to the other five. I missed them all, especially Walter, but curiously the one I missed most was the first child to come into Coldharbour after Milo appeared overhead—his little sister, Jenny. Strange, because I'd only known her for a few hours before we parted, and I didn't normally make friends with younger kids.

My beauty, though, led me away from her. Milo himself had told me that a second generation of child defenders would be arriving who needed my beauty as much as he had. For hours now, led by it, I'd been wandering vaguely along the eastern perimeter of Coldharbour, expecting to discover them.

I didn't have much to go on. Just an image, a picture in my mind. A picture of a boy. No ordinary boy, though. He frightened me, this one. After Milo, I'd hoped that the next child who needed my beauty would be easier to help, but now I wasn't so sure. The first time I'd seen Milo swish out of the darkness on his deformed hands had been bad, but at least Milo had possessed hands. At least Milo had fingers on those hands, even if they were falling to pieces.

The new child my beauty sought had no fingers. No fingers or thumbs. No true hands at all.

"You all right there?"

A teenage girl on the other side of the street, maybe twelve or thirteen years old, was calling out to me. Two small boys clung to her skirt. I couldn't resist glancing at their hands. Fingers and thumbs as normal.

"I'm fine," I said. "Those your brothers?"

"They behave like it," she said ruefully. "I found them about an hour ago. Been traveling ages, obviously. God knows where they're from."

"Why not give them over to a child-family?"

"Yeah, I would—" she laughed, "but they won't let go of me. I think they came in with an older sister, and lost her somewhere on the way."

Gazing at the teenager, I realized that she'd already become an adoptive mother to the boys. Part of me wanted to help her get them safely into Coldharbour. Another part let her go on her way. These toddlers weren't the reason I was here.

This morning my beauty expected to greet the handless boy.

I wished the girl luck and wandered aimlessly around the territory on the outskirts of Coldharbour for a while longer. I passed a house with a motion-detector alarm blaring away. It had probably been triggered by a child running out of the house. No one had bothered to shut it off.

Then, like a promise, my beauty stirred.

Instantly I forgot about everything else, and allowed myself to be guided into Coldharbour's northwest region. I'd never visited this area before, but it was the same as everywhere else, packed with children standing around in the mud. I stepped gingerly around their feet, until I came to a place where the crowds thinned. Heading that way, I knew at once that my beauty had found what it was looking for.

In a gap—all together and separate from everyone else—were about two hundred children.

The first thing I noticed was the stones. Coldharbour is basically barren earth, but here there were rocks everywhere: old hunks of brick, shards of flint, even slabs of concrete that must have been hauled from miles away.

As soon as you saw the stones you understood why everyone in Coldharbour had given these particular children so much space to themselves. At first I thought the children were just lying on or sitting against the stones. Then I saw them rubbing them against their bodies. Each child had its own personal stone, as if it had a favorite. One girl close to me was dragging a flint across her face. She did it slowly, from one side to the other. It was one of the most disturbing things I'd ever seen.

I hesitated to get any closer, but my beauty was sure.

I checked their hands.

Nothing unusual there. Fingers intact. I knew something surprising was about to happen, though, because as soon as I arrived all of the rock-children stopped what they were doing and turned towards me. One boy caught my attention. It was his chin that struck me first: square and blunt, no-nonsense. Apart from that, he had high cheekbones, straight severely cropped hair, and a solid build. There was definitely something impressive about him. His hair was blond, though you could hardly tell, it was so filthy. Anyone could see that he and the others had been rubbing their bodies about in the mud. Their faces were caked in it. They smelled of soil and crushed stone.

"Hi," I said, as casually as I could. "I'm . . . my name's Thomas."

"Tanni," said the blond-haired boy, nodding in acknowledgement. He gestured at the rest of them. "Meet the Unearthers."

"The what?"

"The Unearthers." He smiled. "Since we got here we spend all our time grubbing about in the earth. We've no idea why. It's as good a name as we can come up with."

I had no idea what to say to that. Tanni continued to stare at me, then walked over and held out a fragment of stone.

"You want some of this?"

"No."

"You sure?" His gray-blue eyes studied me. He edged closer, all the while raking the stone against his forehead. The Unearthers, I thought. Eerie name.

"Why are you doing that?" I asked.

"Doing what?"

"Pulling that across your head."

He drew the stone away from his brow.

"Better than food," Tanni said, as if that answer made perfect sense. He approached me, coming right up to my face, and I took a couple of steps back. "Don't," he said, his voice wavering.

"Don't what?"

"Don't . . . I don't know. Don't leave us."

Even if I'd wanted to, there was no chance of that; the remaining Unearthers had already surrounded me. I tried to keep my composure. Hadn't my beauty led me to these children? There had to be a reason.

"Do *you* know why we're all scraping rocks over our skin?" Tanni asked.

"No," I said. "Sorry. I've . . . no idea."

He moved closer, gazing into my eyes as if the answer might be there. His stare was unsettling and I considered trying to put some distance between us, but it was too late for that—the other Unearthers had blocked off any sight of the rest of Coldharbour. I instinctively looked around, prepared to shout for help if I had to.

"Don't worry," Tanni said, "we're not going to harm you. In fact, I think we've been waiting for you, Thomas."

"Oh yeah?" I replied, flustered.

"What led you here?"

"My beauty . . . but I don't know why."

"Your beauty?"

The Unearthers gathered around me, cradling their chunks of rock. I felt like running. Trying to stay cool, I reminded myself that it had been far more frightening than this when I first met Milo. I attempted to relax, to accept the creepy presence of the Unearthers, but it wasn't easy.

"We're scaring you," Tanni said. "I'm sorry. We don't mean to. It's just that ever since we came here we've been hanging out with these stones. None of us knows why. You've no idea what it's been like."

"Where did you get the stones from?"

"Wherever we could," Tanni said. "I had to dig way down to get mine. It took ages. Then I had to cut it to get a genuinely keen edge. That took ages as well." He reached out an arm to me. "Can I . . . can I touch you?"

"What?"

"I know it sounds weird. A small touch of your face, that's all."

I swallowed. ". . . Yes."

Tanni put his left hand ever so softly against my cheek.

And that's when it happened. As soon as Tanni made contact with the skin, my beauty erupted. Tanni drew back, clutching his hand, and gazed down. And all the other Unearthers gazed with him, because a change was taking place. At first I couldn't believe what I was seeing. Tanni's knuckles were *growing*. Within seconds they broke from the surface skin of his fingers and rose up. The protruding bones were sharp-edged, not blunt like normal knuckles. Tanni examined his other hand; the same effect was at work.

He stared at me in awe. "How did you do this?"

"My beauty . . ."

The remaining Unearthers abruptly pressed against

me. Each one reached out to touch my exposed skin wherever they could find it: wrists, hands, face, neck. The moment they did so the same sharp bony ridges jutted from their knuckles.

They stared at each other, swishing their hands through the air like knives.

"What's happening?" I whispered.

Tanni shook his head, staring at his hands in disbelief.

A tall, dark-haired girl pushed forward. "My name's Parminder," she announced. "Did you say your beauty's doing this? Is that what you said? Is that what you called it?" She licked her lips. "Will you give me some more?"

I studied my own hands. No bones bursting through, at least. I'd have been surprised if there had been—my beauty was always intended for others. It continued to empty into the Unearthers. A second girl tugged at my sleeve, after more of my skin. I wanted to give her and the others whatever they needed, but they were crowding me too closely.

"What do you want in return for more of your beauty?" one asked.

"I don't want anything," I said. "What are you talking about? Please . . . stop getting so close . . ."

"Are you hungry?" a boy asked, fumbling in his pockets. "Will you give me more beauty for food? I have food. Are you thirsty?"

"Are you cold?" someone else asked. "You can have this." He started taking off his jacket. Others were prepared to hand over different items of clothing or even their precious rocks for a longer feel of my flesh.

Parminder groped for my face. She put her palm against my forehead. Then she lunged forward and kissed me. I screamed, and Tanni pulled her away from me.

"Just leave Thomas alone!" he shouted. "What's the matter with you all?" His hand was cold. It shook as he held it over my mouth. Crouching on the ground to get away from all the arms, I looked up at Parminder. Her kiss hadn't been friendly or unfriendly; more of an experiment. She prodded her lips afterwards, feeling with interest for any changes there.

"Everyone calm down," Tanni growled. "Give Thomas room to breathe. Back off. Allow him some space! Can't you see he's just as scared as the rest of us?"

He removed his hand from my mouth. As he drew it away the knuckle of his thumb changed again. It lengthened. It thickened.

And then, without warning, the Roar slipped through my mind like a spike. I'd never heard it so deafening, and all the children in Coldharbour, including the Unearthers, wailed with pain.

Tanni and several of the other Unearthers immediately formed a guarding circle around me. Their sharpened hands were held outward.

"Protect him!" Tanni commanded them.

the child city

HELEN

"It's incredible, Helen," Dad whispered.

We stood together in the early dawn light, watching children of all ages racing each other into Coldharbour.

"How many are coming?" he asked me, shaking his head in awe. "Do you know?"

"They're all coming," I told him.

"What? Every child in the world?"

"Yes. If they can."

Dad tightened his arm around me. He stood six foot three in his walking boots, towering over nearly all those around us except the largest of the teenagers. The only adult in Coldharbour, I thought. A single father who made it in—and only because he was here before the Barrier appeared. With his powerful build and thinning hair Dad looked strangely out of place and vulnerable to me in this emerging child city.

"What about kids too ill to travel?" he asked. "There

must be some like that. Children in hospitals. Or ones who can't walk."

"Others will carry them," I said.

"And what if an ocean stands between a child and Coldharbour?"

I gazed up at him. "That'll only delay them, Dad. They'll find a way across eventually. If there's time, that is. If they can reach us before the Roar gets here."

Dad squeezed my arm, thinking, *How long will that be?*

"I don't know," I admitted. "Not long, though. It's nearly here."

Standing beside him, I reached out for the thoughts of all children across the world. In China millions were on the move. Those lucky enough to be able to steal vehicles or auto-rickshaws were heading recklessly towards the nearest shorelines. The remainder traveled by bike or on foot. Further east still, the sun shone down on children congregating at two of Japan's great seaports, Yokohama and Kitakyushu. Each child was frantically trying to get aboard a ship or anything that might float to take them west.

I could read all their minds.

I hadn't always been able to do that. Until recently, only the minds of the closest people and animals were open to me. Not any longer. Shortly after Milo flew above us, I was exposed to the thoughts of every single adult and child on the Earth. And it led to this—heart-lurches suddenly drawing my mind everywhere. I gripped Dad's hand as the latest one took me to northern Russia. Two brothers there, trying to reach us, were attempting to cross the Volga River. After heavy rains the river was in full flood, and neither boy was a strong swimmer.

Dad felt me shiver. "What is it? Are you cold?"

"No, it's not that. It's just . . . some children won't make it, that's all."

Dad stared at me. "Can't you screen out these thoughts, Helen? You won't make their journeys any easier. You'll be a wreck if you don't find a way to shut them out."

Dad was right, but it was hard. The children who hadn't yet made it to Coldharbour were all desperate, and the adults, especially the mothers and fathers stuck outside the Barrier, cut off from their children, were almost worse. I could hardly bear to look into their minds at all.

Dad leaned closer to me, and for a while we stood watching Coldharbour's new population arrive. Nearby, a largish group of youngsters were huddled together, staring silently up at Milo.

"Why are they doing that?" Dad asked.

"Because they're happy," I said. "They made it here."

"They trust Milo, don't they?"

"It's more than that. He makes them feel safe. For now, at least."

Dad gazed at a small boy sitting cross-legged in the mud. "I'd expect a lot more noise," he said. "Especially from the little kids. But they're almost calm, aren't they? So quiet, too."

Dad might have had trouble understanding the reason, but none of the children did. After all, we were only waiting. We were waiting, in fact, for the arrival of the new defenders—the second generation of defenders Milo had told us would emerge to stand with him against the Roar.

But where were they? For me it was bitter not knowing, because I was supposed to. Hadn't Milo told me I would help nurture the next generation of defenders? Hadn't he said I'd know what gifts they had, and what to do for them?

But I didn't. I couldn't even find any gifts. Either the new children in Coldharbour had no gifts—or they were being hidden from me. I say hidden, because I'd had a tantalizing glimpse. Just for a moment, when Milo first swept up into the sky, and I'd stood alongside Thomas, we'd both felt a hint of incredible powers. Something astounding in the children rushing towards us. A tremendous potential. Gifts beyond belief.

But that wondrous feeling had been snatched away—abruptly, like a slammed door. Or, rather, like a door prevented from opening. I'd thought of summer. It felt like summer held back; like a shutter composed of winter holding out the sun.

Thomas, nudged by his beauty, had said his farewells to us shortly afterwards. Since then I'd followed his mind across Coldharbour. Until this happened: just before dawn, I lost contact. One moment I was reading Thomas's thoughts clearly; the next there was nothing.

Something had taken him away from me.

And no matter how hard I tried to find his mind, I couldn't.

I shivered again, and Dad put his own jacket around my shoulders.

"Hey, this might cheer you up," he said, pointing southwards. "The twins are on their way back from the dumps."

Emily and Freda approached in their usual manner—skittering along on the balls of their hands and feet—and I smiled. It was frightening when you first met them, all that speed heading towards you in a blur of legs and arms, but you soon became accustomed to it. This was the twins' particular gift: to move about on all fours, seeking out special children. They'd found me that way, and Thomas, and Walter, bringing the first generation of children together.

As I watched them, I realized that I still hadn't figured out exactly how they ran. They moved with elegant, deft movements, their nails barely touching the ground, somehow managing to keep the hems of their dresses out of the mud. Even after a night's work showing other children how to navigate around the rubbish dumps, they both looked amazingly clean.

"Better eat this," Dad muttered, handing me the last

cheese sandwich left from yesterday's journey into Cold-harbour. "Before the twins try tempting you with something else."

"We 'eard that!" Freda said, dashing towards him.

"Got this for yer," Emily said, thrusting a formless gray substance into Dad's hand.

"What is it?" he asked, with deep suspicion.

"Well, it ain't fish and chips, matey," she said, rolling her eyes. "But you can eat it. Powdered eggs. Only been at the dump about a day. Luxury. Go on. Taste it. It won't hurt yer." When Dad hesitated, Emily folded her arms, flicked her long red hair over her shoulders, and said, "Close yer eyes and think of it as a steak."

"If I'd a steak," Freda said, smacking her lips, "I'd eat it."

"If I'd a steak," Emily replied, "I'd slap you with it."

Both girls laughed, while the children around us watched them in bemusement. Dad reluctantly tasted the eggs.

"There," Emily said, patting his arm, "not too bad, eh?" She bent closer, so only Dad could hear what she said next. "It'd 'elp if you put a better look on yer face about it, though. There's kids all round scared to eat this stuff, but what else is there for 'em? Do uz a favor, and smile while you're putting it past yer lips. Being older, all that grey hair on yer head, the kids'll trust you better than uz."

She winked at him, and Dad swallowed the eggs with as much of a smile as he could manage.

Near us, a huge boy stood over a teenage girl. She'd been clinging onto him ever since she found out he was willing to help her and her three brothers.

"N-no problem," he said to her. "I c-can do that for you. You need these f-f-f . . ." A sigh and a pause. "You need these planks of wood f-for f-f-f-foundations. What you d-do is, you p-put them in like this . . ."

It was Walter, of course.

"See, l-like this," he said to the girl, plunging the planks into the ground. He'd spent ages striding all around Coldharbour finding the wood and some nails to start building a hut for her. She had no idea.

"Don't you need a hammer to do that?" she asked, biting her lower lip.

"Nah . . . I g-got these." Walter held up his fingers, using them to press the nails into a couple of sticks. "I'll m-make a roof as well," he said. "But first the f-foundations have to be finished, so—"

"What about clean clothes?" the girl said. "We'll definitely need those, too."

"Clean cl-clothes?" Even Walter nearly laughed at that, and I had to smile. Only a couple of hours ago this girl had run shrieking from Walter when she first saw him. You couldn't blame her. We'd all got used to the twelve-foot tallness and five-foot width of him, but Walter was a sight to behold the first time he loomed over you.

"I'll t-try to find clothes for you," Walter said, giving her his best lopsided smile. "I think I m-might be able to."

She smiled back at him as if he were her own brother.

"Better go to his rescue," Dad muttered to me. "That girl's practically adopted him. She'll have Walter hunting for fluffy carpets if we don't watch out."

Dad was right. Walter couldn't say no to anyone. In the night I'd found him playing hide-and-seek with a little girl. She'd just turned up, tapped that massive shin of his, and asked him. The girl became one of what Walter called his "visitors." Lots of these had arrived in the night—small children who wanted to be near him. Now that dawn was spreading a little light across Coldharbour, you could see a whole troop of them following him about. I knew why. They wanted to stay close to Walter, that's all. You didn't need to be a mind reader to understand why. Everyone who met him did. We all instinctively knew that when the Roar arrived the safest place to find yourself would be in Walter's arms.

He was particularly beset this morning, because while several youngsters were running about his feet and generally getting in his way, Emily had jumped on him, too. Being fastidiously neat herself, she found it hard to bear Walter's unkempt sandy hair sticking out in all directions. Climbing up his body, she perched on his neck. In her hands there was a huge rusty comblike object. I think at one time it belonged to a garden rake. For about ten minutes I watched her dragging it across Walter's scalp, without making much impression. "You're so untidy, Walts," she moaned in his ear. "Your hair's all over! Why don't yer let me cut it? You'll look much better . . . you know I'm right. . . ."

Walter ignored her, hardly aware she was on him. Freda was also scampering around Walter's heels, measuring them up. Ever since she'd met him weeks ago she'd been trying to make something that would stay on his outsized feet.

Walter let the twins hang off him while he finished part of the teenage girl's hut. He used one arm for this. His other arm was occupied by a titchy boy tucking himself under his armpit.

Emily laughed. "Find out how to carry a kid under yer arm!" she announced.

"Find out how to go mad and stay calm!" Freda added.

Walter had constructed his own hut in the night. It was a roomy dwelling, bolted together from wood, plastic, and steel he found on the dumps. "A place for my visitors," he'd informed us. One of those was calling out to him now. She let out a piercing, high-pitched screech.

"G-got to g-go," Walter told the teenage girl. "B-be back soon."

"But—" she held onto him—"what about my other things? You said—"

"S-sorry. I'll get them later. G-got to go see to Jenny."

Another high-pitched screech.

Jenny was Milo's five-year-old sister. She had lengthy mid-brown hair framing a slim, rather serious face, but that's not what you noticed most about her. What you noticed was her fixation with Walter. Jenny wanted to spend every single second with him. She'd clung to him for much of the night and now, only two minutes after waking up, she was stamping her feet, already impatient for his attention again. Rubbing sleep out of her eyes, she threaded her way across to him, nudging smaller children out of the way.

She tugged at his trousers. "Didn't you hear us?" she demanded. "Didn't you? We've been waiting."

She held up her stone doll, Agatha. Jenny had come into Coldharbour with a rag doll, but this was her new favorite. With a bit of help from Dad in the night, Jenny had made the doll herself. She stood there, poking Agatha crossly at Walter. Then Jenny squinted up at Milo. She smiled, giving him a friendly wave.

Jenny was a mystery to me. Not just an ordinary little girl; I was sure of that. I'd seen the way Thomas had been drawn to her at once. There was something remarkable about her, though I had no idea what.

"Walter doesn't like that!" she wailed, attempting to drag out the tiny boy ensconced in Walter's armpit. The boy, however, wasn't about to let go of his place without a fight. He clung onto Walter like a gibbon. Unable to bash him into submission, Jenny instead glared moodily at Emily.

A jealous little thing, Jenny was. She wanted Walter all to herself.

"Where were you?" she complained, smacking his

shins. "You weren't there when we woke up. We didn't know where you were."

With a finger and thumb, Walter picked Jenny up. He twirled her in the air. "H-h-hungry?"

Jenny made Agatha nod.

"W-want a surprise?"

Another nod.

"Close y-your eyes then."

Jenny dropped Agatha without a thought, scrunched up her lids and held out both hands. "A treat," Walter said, placing half a biscuit in each one. Jenny giggled, eating them fast, then gripped Walter's trousers to make sure he didn't walk off again. The twins offered her some more food they'd brought from the dumps.

Jenny ate it absentmindedly. She wasn't interested in eating. Reading her mind, I noticed unusual thoughts passing through her head. Something to do with her hands. She inspected her fingers with great care, especially the knuckles. She rubbed them a few times. Then, frowning, she picked up Agatha again.

Considering that she was only a hunk of rock, Agatha was fairly pretty. The face was neatly etched, with nice eyes, a proper-shaped nose and a big smiley mouth. For hair, there were wavy streaks carved down the sides of her head. Jenny inspected Agatha critically for some time. Then she picked up a sharp piece of flint and cut into one of the doll's hands. She spent a while on this, humming quietly to herself, patiently jabbing and poking away.

Walter tried to see what she was doing.

"Not finished yet!" Jenny chided, concealing her work.

The twins sneaked behind her.

"What yer doing, Jens?" Freda asked. "Don't yer like Agatha the way she was?"

"I'm not finished yet!" Jenny hid Agatha against her tummy, covering her up. Then, dissatisfied with her work, she changed the way she held the flint. Holding it now like a knife, she struck down as hard as she could on Agatha's hands.

"J-Jenny!" Walter went to snatch the doll away.

I caught his eye. "No, let her finish."

"B-but, Helen, she might hurt herself. She—"

"Let her finish, Walter!"

Our closest neighbors all stopped whatever they were doing and studied the strange little girl hacking at her dolly. Jenny didn't care. She was entirely focused on Agatha. Chip-chip, she chopped away at her hands.

"There," Jenny said, blowing rock-dust off Agatha's face. "See!"

Walter examined the doll for a moment, then showed us.

It wasn't the same Agatha. Her face was the same, but where were her hands? Jenny had sliced them off. I'd seen her do it with two quick cuts of the flint. On the stumps, where the doll's hands should have been, Jenny had engraved minute details. Walter, Dad, and the twins all tried to understand what the sharp, bladelike parts were meant to be.

"Like cutters," Emily murmured. "Like teeth. Is that what they are, Jens?"

Jenny shook her head. Then she grabbed Agatha back from Walter and threw her hard against the ground. "I hate you!" she cried. "I hate you!" She stamped over and over on Agatha's head, grinding it into the dirt. "If I'd a rock," she shouted, "I'd split it! If I'd a rock, I'd hit it!" She stared at Emily and Freda, challenging them to outdo her—but for once the twins had nothing to add.

Walter tried to calm her down. "Jenny, It's all r-right. She's just a d-doll. She c-can't hurt you."

Dad walked over to Agatha. He picked her up, cleaned the mud from her hand-stumps and showed them to me. "Are they teeth, Helen?"

"No," I said. "They're not teeth, Dad."

I studied the tiny marks on the doll's stumps. They looked superficially like teeth, and that's what I'd have guessed they were if I hadn't checked into Jenny's mind. But when I looked there I saw they weren't teeth at all.

They were drills.

THREE

a grave for a bed

THOMAS

"They're still growing," Tanni said. "Thomas, what on earth is happening to us?"

Throughout the morning the knuckles of the Unearthers had continued to change. At first they were shaped like blades, poking straight up through the skin. Then they began to curve around. In half the children the knuckles curved to the left; in the rest to the right.

All of them were terrified. Tanni was clearly their natural leader, and he did his best to keep the rest of the Unearthers calm, yet even he couldn't stop staring at his hands, waiting for the next development. I had no idea what that might be, but my beauty obviously wanted to go inside these children, and I trusted in that. After all, this wasn't the first disfigured child my beauty had helped bring into being. Milo's hands, too, had been deformed until the moment they spread out to become the buttresses for his wings.

I told the Unearthers about this and, needing reassurance, they clung to every word I said. Some of the smallest children even started running around with outstretched arms, thinking they were transforming into miniature Milos. The older ones were harder to convince. I'd never seen teenagers look so scared. They stood around in small groups, holding their stones for comfort, trying to come to some acceptance of what they were turning into. Some couldn't stop staring at their hands; the rest didn't want to look at all.

Tanni was as nervous as any of them but, knowing the other Unearthers were seeking a crumb of confidence anywhere they could find it, he attempted to keep a neutral expression and hold his nerve. In private, though, showing me his knuckles, he trembled.

"Always larger, bent and twisted," he said. "Like horror-things. Do you think our knuckles are becoming weapons, Thomas?"

I considered that. Was my beauty creating weapons out of the hands of these children?

"No, they're too small to be weapons," Tanni decided.

"They're sharp enough," I said.

"Maybe," Tanni replied. "We're not like Milo, though, eh? You said he had flaking skin and lost some fingers. That's not happening to us. See the way the knuckles are bent? It's a precise curve, exactly the same for each knuckle—as if a machine's made them. And what do you think of this?" He rapped his fingers against a piece of flint, part of which chipped off. "See that? See how hard the bones are becoming? Normal bones can't do anything like that. But—" he swallowed—"it's okay, isn't it? I mean, your beauty's doing this. We have to trust it."

"I don't know what's happening to you," I said, holding his gaze, "but I know this much: Milo said my beauty would prepare the way for the second set of defenders. And he told us those defenders would be children."

"Yes." Tanni nodded several times, as if trying to convince himself. "That's what we are. Not new Milos, but something to stand alongside him." He glanced around. "There are a lot of us, Thomas. I've counted. Exactly two hundred and four Unearthers. Makes you think, doesn't it? If Milo needs all our help, how big is the Roar going to be?"

I had no answer to that, but I was anxious to encourage him in some way. "The knuckles aren't such a big change," I said.

Tanni gave me a look. "Thomas, I'm not a little kiddy, you know. You don't need to pretend or hold my hand or anything. Besides, it's not what's happened so far that bothers me most. These knuckles aren't pretty, but I can live with that. It's what's to come. See the size of Milo? I can't believe we're going stay the way we are now. I reckon these knuckles are just the beginning of bigger changes to us. And I've been thinking about something else, too. Our parents. Where are they?"

"Behind the Barrier."

"Yes, but why's the Barrier there? I come from the north. My parents drove all night to get here. They only had to take one look at my face to see there was no point trying to stop me. And they wanted to stay with me, too. But they couldn't, could they."

"You know the reason they're stuck outside?" I asked.

"No. But I think it's because of what's to come."

"Go on."

"I'm not sure, but I don't think it's going to be safe for adults in Coldharbour. I reckon they're being kept out for their own protection. I think we're heading for places adults can't follow. Dangerous places. Especially us. Especially the Unearthers. I've had that feeling from the start. Well?" he said, staring challengingly up at me. "What's next, Thomas? Where's that beauty of yours taking us?"

I had no idea, but we didn't have to wait long to find out. The first of the big changes to the Unearthers occurred shortly after midday.

It had been warming up all morning, the sun glistening off the sea, with hardly a breeze except that billowing from the underside of Milo's left wing. For hours the Unearthers had been sitting around, attempting to figure out what to do with their misshapen knuckles. What took place next seemed ordinary at first. One of the Unearthers—a boy—simply slipped up. Nothing strange about that, but Coldharbour's well-trodden mud caught him out and he fell awkwardly. He didn't have enough time to put out his arms to break his fall.

He fell, the whole weight of him, face-first, on a slab of concrete.

Seeing it happen I winced, waiting for the inevitable howl of pain. It didn't come. Only the sound of a head whacking concrete. I've no idea what it normally sounds like when a boy's head does that, but this sound definitely wasn't it. The noise was hollow, like two solid objects colliding.

I didn't know what to make of it, but the reaction of the other Unearthers was interesting: they stopped whatever they were doing and turned to the boy. He'd picked himself up from the ground and was standing there, rubbing his nose gingerly with his forearm, an expression of surprise on his face. There wasn't a scratch on him. The concrete slab hadn't fared so favorably. It lay shattered in several pieces beside him.

"Well, well," said Tanni.

And this is what he did next. He picked out the biggest, thickest hunk of rock he could find, straightened his shoulders and rammed his face fully against it.

There was that ringing note again, like iron on stone.

I shuddered, but Tanni smiled, clapping a hand on my shoulder. "It's all right," he said. "I didn't feel a thing."

A few of the braver Unearthers immediately began testing their faces in the same way. Then a boy picked out a girl. She was a toddler, his sister I think. Seeing what he was about to do, I tried to intervene, but Tanni stopped me. That little girl. Her head looked so fragile, glistening with perspiration in the sunshine. She crouched down. Planting her feet firmly in the soil, she pulled the fringe off her brow. "Here?" she questioned the boy, touching her head where she expected the impact to be. He nodded, and ran towards her. He did it at full speed. At the last moment he lowered his head, aiming just above her eyes.

I couldn't watch. The impact was like metal on metal. The air chimed. Silence followed, and I opened one eye. The boy and girl were nowhere near each other. The violence of the impact had knocked them far apart. But they were both uninjured.

They grinned at one another across the mud.

Before long Tanni had persuaded some of the more daring Unearthers to have a go at copying the boy and girl. The rest weren't so eager to try, but after plenty of encouragement and cajoling Tanni finally had most of them lined up, getting their foreheads into position. It was weird watching them, all those sweaty heads crunching into each other, their skulls ringing like bells in the afternoon sunshine.

Later that day, though, all mirth came to an abrupt end once the Unearthers realized something: it wasn't only the surface of their faces that was as hard as metal. Their appearance remained the same, but underneath, under the skin, every part of them started to have a firm, unbreakable feel. Tanni noticed it first, but by the late afternoon every one of the Unearthers knew that they didn't have a single soft spot left on their bodies.

"Jab my eyes," Tanni said. "Go on."

I wouldn't, so he took my finger and prodded his eyeball. It was completely hard. So were the eyelids. Tanni's jaw, when I felt it, was solid steel. His eyelashes stuck out like iron spikes. His tongue, when he rolled it past his lips, was like a knife.

This was too much for the Unearthers to take—too much too quickly. Sharp knuckles were one thing, but they couldn't cope with knives. There were tears and near breakdowns. I think the only thing that enabled them to keep a slender grip on their minds at all was that they still looked the same. Except for their hands, the Unearthers still looked human.

But were they? I don't know what made me question it, but I suddenly did. What came after beauty? The beast, of course. I shrugged that frightening thought away, but it kept returning, and the more it did the more I wished Helen was here to tell me what on earth was going on inside the minds of these children. I felt certain she must be reading my thoughts, and that if there was anything I needed to know she'd find a way for Walter to get a message to me. But I still couldn't relax about it. Was my beauty trying to warn me about the Unearthers—or alert me to something threatening them?

Whatever was in store, Tanni was fantastic over the next few hours. Throughout the evening he tirelessly checked on the Unearthers, finding words of reassurance for everyone. Watching him, I realized that he'd taken the trouble to learn many of their individual names. That was useful now, as he wandered amongst the groups. To occupy the youngsters in the evening he came up with special tasks—measure each other's knuckles, scrape at the soil, anything to keep them busy. The teenagers were a bigger challenge, and Tanni didn't pretend he had any answers for them, but he never showed them how apprehensive he was. Only I saw that when we chatted alone.

Late that evening he returned to sit with me, exhausted.

"Metal faces," he muttered. "Metal legs, metal arms, everything as hard as metal. What's next, Thomas?" He shook his head. "This had better be the worst stage, because I'm running out of ideas to hold us together."

"You're doing a brilliant job," I told him, meaning it. "The Unearthers are all listening to you. Don't be so hard on yourself."

He grinned wryly. "Brilliant, eh? I'm not so sure. I've started awarding points to the first youngster who notices the next new development. Seemed like a good idea—get them looking forward to the changes instead of scared to death. Is that a brilliant idea?"

"It'll work anyway," I said. "It makes sense to keep them occupied. You've got their trust, I'll tell you that."

Tanni rolled his eyes. "I'm wetting my pants here, Thomas. I've half-convinced the youngsters everything's some kind of ridiculous game, but they're not stupid. I've no idea how they're going to react to the next set of changes."

I wanted to say, "Maybe there won't be any more changes." But I didn't, because I didn't believe it, and I knew Tanni wouldn't, either.

He suddenly stared up at Milo. "Well?" he asked.

I knew what Tanni was hoping for. He wanted to hear an approving whisper from those giant lips, a sign, any sign, that this was what Milo wanted. But there was no reaction from the silver child, and when I put my hand on Tanni's shoulder to reassure him his hands started to shake. When the shaking became visible, he hid them.

"It's all right," I said. "No one's looking." I edged closer to him, partially shielding him from view. "Listen, Tanni, I've been thinking. Maybe all this is happening too fast. I've been letting my beauty flow as freely into you as it wants. Maybe I should slow it down."

"No. Don't do that."

"But look at you all!"

"Is the Roar slowing down?" Tanni gripped my arm fiercely. "Well? Do you think it is? I don't know how long we've got before it gets here, but not long. And when it does we'd better be ready. No, let your beauty do what it wants, Thomas. Don't control it. Let it go. Let it pour into us."

The most startling change so far took place in the Unearthers less than an hour later, and Tanni was the first to feel its effects. I'm not sure why it was him. Perhaps because he'd touched me first. Perhaps because he'd been closer to me than the rest of the Unearthers. In any case, when it started even Tanni lost all his composure.

"Thomas! What are you doing to me?"

His fingers were shortening. No, it was worse than that—they were *dissolving*. It was as if acid was on them. The tips and the nails were already gone. Tanni tried to keep his voice under control. "I'm losing my fingers. I can't lose my fingers!"

Moments later, the other children started to scream when they experienced the same changes.

Taking a deep breath, Tanni stood up so they could all see him.

"Stay calm," he said loudly. "Everyone listen to me. There's no pain. What's happening to your hands . . . has already happened to me, and it doesn't hurt." His words didn't stop the Unearthers from screaming, but they heard him, and realized it was true.

Tanni's fingers dissolved completely down to the stubs. Raising his hands for the rest to see, he kept his voice steady. "It's all right! No matter what it looks like, there's still no pain."

"How can it be all right?" said a voice.

It was Parminder, the dark-haired girl who'd surprised me with that kiss the first time I met the Unearthers.

She'd apologized about that, and she'd been great earlier in the day, too, helping Tanni get to know the rest of the girls amongst the Unearthers. But I'd noticed she was a willful character; Parminder was quick to let you know what she thought, and this latest transformation outraged her.

"It's not all right!" she shouted. "We're losing our hands! How can that be all right?"

"No, that's not true," Tanni said. "I don't think so. Only the fingers. And look . . ."

The last remnants of Tanni's fingers and thumbs dropped away. As soon as they did, his palms began to widen. Soon they were twice the size of a normal child's palms. Then they were twice the size of an adult's. The shape also altered. They became circular. And at the end of the circular hands, like a ring of steel, were the machine-precise knuckles.

"Like saws," a boy suggested.

"Or drills," someone else said.

A buzz of excitement immediately cut across the fear of the Unearthers, and within minutes the transformation of their hands had come to an end. Each child now had drill-like parts around the edges of immense-sized hands. Parminder held them away from her body in disgust.

"Well, what do we do now?" she yelled. "Look at the state of us!"

"We wait," Tanni said, uncertainly. "We'll get used to this, just as we got used to the previous changes."

"Get used to them?" Parminder cried. "How can we get used to them? We can't even eat now! How can we eat without fingers?"

"We'll find a way."

"That's ridiculous! There isn't a way!"

Tanni stared at her. "Look, we will. How does a dog eat? How does a four-legged animal eat? We'll eat like them if we have to."

"Like beasts?" Parminder demanded. "Is that what you mean? Is that what we are now, then? Beasts?"

"No, of course not," Tanni said. "Look at the shape of your hands. They're drills, I'm sure of it. And what do you do with a drill?"

"You dig," someone shouted.

"That's right!" Tanni lowered his hands, leaning into the soil below.

Nothing happened. Tanni had sounded so confident that for a moment I think even Parminder believed his hands would start churning up the mud. When they didn't, Tanni couldn't hide his disappointment. He cleared his throat. "We're just not ready yet," he said. "We're nearly complete, I'm sure. There . . . there can't be many more alterations to go now."

Some didn't believe him, but they all wanted to. They desperately needed to trust in something.

Twilight settled in, Milo brightened in the late evening sky, and the Unearthers waited for more changes. As the

49

evening arrived, most of them withdrew into their own private worlds of fear, staring with loathing at their drill-hands.

"Surely you must have some idea where this is heading," Tanni said to me.

But I didn't. I had no idea at all. And did it feel right? Did it? I kept asking myself what my beauty was doing to these children, and I got no answers whatsoever.

Twilight became night, and Milo burned more brightly to compensate. Projecting a smooth shadowless radiance over everyone in Coldharbour, he lowered his wing to ward off a stiff breeze coming in off the sea. The Unearthers didn't notice the weather change. Wrapped up in their own transformation, they didn't show much interest in the new children entering Coldharbour, either. As night came on, Parminder and several others clumsily collected a few scraps of food. The Unearthers ate it as best they could. Afterwards, to keep the teenagers occupied, Tanni got them to settle the youngsters down for the night.

No nice comfy beds for these kids. No blankets. No soft mattresses or yielding pillows. Their new bodies wanted only one thing: hardness, edges, the feel of rock. To get comfortable that night the Unearthers had to pack stones tightly up against their bodies. Even then they got no peace, because a strange thing kept happening—whenever they fell asleep, they would move towards each other. It was weird. Their sleeping bodies kept wriggling across the soil until they touched.

With hands as sharp as theirs that was dangerous. Despite their metal bones, Tanni didn't want to take the risk of a sleeping face brushing accidentally against one of the knuckles.

With all the Unearthers watching him, Tanni scooped a hollow in the earth. He scraped and gouged at the soil until the hollow was deep and wide enough to place his body inside. It was like an open grave.

"At least if we do this we can sleep," Tanni said to them all.

The youngsters copied him, delving away with their new hands, and soon, after all the exertions of the day, the majority were sleeping fitfully. The older Unearthers were too anxious to sleep, and most didn't bother trying. I listened to their conversations. I also listened to the other sounds they made. From time to time, whenever they were near each other, their bodies would accidentally touch. It kept on happening. Little clicking noises. Little metallic taps. It was like a prickly murmur around me all night.

At some point in the small hours, Tanni bedded down in his own hole. He wasn't able to lie on his front—his mouth would have been in the mud—so he settled instead on his back, facing Milo. With his drill-hands tight by his side, he lay there restlessly, staring up wide-eyed at the stars shining dully between Milo's wings.

What strange tough children was my beauty bringing

into the world?

At some point I drifted off to sleep myself, but I was soon awakened by a voice. It belonged to one of the young Unearthers near me. I propped myself up to see what was wrong with him. He was dreaming. The poor boy was lying in his little open grave of a bed, softly calling out Milo's name over and over.

FOUR

the lure of the sea

HELEN

Just after mid-morning, someone's nightmare made me scream.

I'd lost count of how many nightmares had streaked through my mind since dawn. All kinds of nightmares: drifting-off-to-sleep ones and those of exhausted children lying at all angles in Coldharbour's mud. I'd tried throughout the morning to doze through them, but I kept flinching awake, disturbing the twins. They lay on their mattress, close to me. Emily's freckled arms were around Freda's. They were so tightly wrapped up together that I could barely tell whose thin hand was uppermost in the tangle above the blanket.

"Sorry about that," I whispered. "You might want to try sleeping somewhere else." I managed a grin. "Somewhere quieter."

Emily fumbled for my hand. "Helen," she said, "if I could stay awake for you, I'd do it."

"If you could have my sleep," Freda added, "I'd give it."

"I know you would." I reached out to them both, and we lay quietly like that for a time.

"Still nothing from Toms?" Emily asked anxiously.

"No," I answered. "I wish there was. I've no idea what's happening to him."

Deciding to leave the twins in peace, I got up, tucked my already grubby blouse into my jeans and ventured outside. Dad was nearby, cleaning out a makeshift latrine. He'd been close enough to hear my latest scream and, knowing the cause, was fighting off an urge to run around waking up everyone in Coldharbour. No chance of that, of course. Only the Roar, when it chose to raise its voice, had that power.

"Can I get you anything?" he asked, wrapping his jacket across my shoulders.

"No, I'm okay."

He put his arms around me, and we sat together watching all the children still entering Coldharbour. So many. And everywhere you looked the youngest were gazing raptly up at Milo.

"I've been thinking," I said.

"Oh?"

"About Agatha."

Dad shuddered. "What kind of a doll is she, Helen? Cutting off her hands wasn't the worst thing Jenny did to her, either. Did you see what she did afterwards?"

"Yes. I'm afraid I did."

I could hardly believe what Jenny had done to her doll. Right after finishing Agatha's hands and kicking her in the mud, she had picked her up and totally wrecked her. Poor Agatha. No more smiley mouth. No more pretty features. Jenny had rubbed them off with a stone, completely disfigured her. She didn't even leave Agatha with a proper girl's face. She'd taken rough hold of her, rubbed out her nose, cut off her lips, scratched dents in her head and scraped away all her hair. It was appalling.

I'd tried talking to Jenny about why she'd done it yesterday, and got nothing from her. Time to try again.

Leaving Dad's side, I made my way between children to Walter's hut. He heard my footsteps, and reached out to open the door. Jenny was inside, asleep in his arms. Looking at her, I realized that if it was possible to lie forever bundled up with Walter, sunk quiet and lost in his hands, Jenny would have.

I shook her softly, but she kept her eyes closed, pretending to be asleep. She didn't want me disturbing her private time with Walter.

"Come back later," she told me curtly, when I wouldn't go away. "We're busy. Leave us alone."

"I will," I said, "but first I want you to tell me about something. About your doll. About those drills you gave her." Jenny's eyes flickered briefly open, then closed again.

"The drills were very sharp, weren't they?" I said, keeping my voice light. "What did Agatha need them for?"

Jenny sat up in the bed.

"She wanted to dig."

"Did she? Why?"

"I don't know."

"There must be a reason, Jenny."

"I don't know."

"Agatha wanted to dig so much, didn't she?"

"Yes."

A noise outside distracted Jenny and she turned back to Walter, rubbing her nose against his neck. "I'm tired," she said. "I'm still sleepy."

Looking into Jenny's thoughts, I saw that there was nothing more she was ready to tell me about Agatha. However, something else was lurking in her mind. I sat beside her, stroking her hair, keeping my voice as casual as I could.

"Walter's very tired," Jenny said. "He wants to be left alone with me."

"I'll go in a minute. But first . . . can you tell me why Agatha frightens you so much? She scares you. I know she does. Isn't she just a doll?"

"No," Jenny said firmly. "She's not a doll. She's a real person. She's a girl."

"But girls don't have hands like that."

"Some do."

"Which girls?"

Jenny nestled against Walter for reassurance.

"It's all right," he soothed her. "T-tell Helen everything. It's s-safe to tell her, you know."

But Jenny said nothing more. Despite Walter's coaxing, she merely buried her head in his shoulder, her mind switched away from all thoughts about Agatha or drills. It was only as I turned to leave that she did something. She puckered up her lips. She put them together and made a hissing noise between her small white teeth. Walter thought the noise was meant to represent a snake, but he was wrong.

It was the sound of the sea.

The rest of the morning passed uneventfully, but that afternoon we sent a group out to the Barrier. Some enterprising parents had discovered that while they couldn't cross into Coldharbour themselves, food could be passed through. Ever since, supplies had started trickling into Coldharbour: not quite enough to satisfy our appetites, but enough to stave off any fear of starvation.

Dad asked Walter to go with him, and they set off accompanied by an assortment of youngsters more than willing to carry their share as long as they could stay close to him.

Jenny stayed behind. The twins were surprised, but I understood why. Much as she hated to be parted from Walter, the sound of the sea increasingly dominated her thoughts. In her mind, there was no time to waste.

She was making a new doll.

Freda and Emily scurried nervously across to watch,

but they needn't have worried. It wasn't another horror-Agatha. This time the doll was made from mud. Jenny chatted happily away to herself, gathering up handfuls of mud from the ground. She used her thumbs to shape the doll's body. For the facial features she dug in her nails, softening the mud where she needed to with water.

The twins tried to sneak a look, but Jenny didn't want them to.

"It's not fair!" Emily protested. "Why can't we know what it is?"

"It's not for you," Jenny said matter-of-factly. "It's Walter's birthday present. This isn't the only present I'm giving him. It's just the first present."

Walter's birthday was two days away. He hadn't mentioned it, but I knew, of course. And once I told the twins, everyone else in our area also knew.

Jenny took her time finishing the doll. It was a girl again—a slim girl-doll with skinny arms and flyaway hair. The twins only recognized who it was when Jenny added a dress. There were tiny flower patterns on it.

"Oh, it's Freda!" said Emily.

"Or you," Freda suggested. "It could be you, Emms."

Jenny started at once on the second doll. Eventually both were complete—two identical mud-brown dolls in the image of the twins. I had no idea why Jenny had made them, but she couldn't wait to play with them both. She tried, but they were too wet and slippery, so she propped them up to dry in the afternoon sun.

Within half an hour she was jiggling them up and down on her lap.

"Ah, that's nice, beautiful likenesses," Freda said, watching Jenny play.

Freda would have been more concerned if she'd overheard the chats Jenny was having with the dolls. It was all under Jenny's breath, mostly typical child-talk stuff, but one time she put the dolls' heads together and whispered. It was a long, earnest conversation. No one else could hear what Jenny was saying, but I knew. Pretty-mud-doll-Freda was trying to persuade her sister that they wouldn't drown, wouldn't drown, wouldn't drown.

The day wore on, the sun dropping down under Milo's torso, while Jenny continued to play.

Dad, Walter, and his eager band of hangers-on returned shortly before dusk. They'd managed to obtain enough food, toilet paper, and bottled water to last us a day or so. Miraculously, there was even fresh linen and Emily nearly squawked with joy when Walter gave her a bar of lemon soap. The twins fought over it a moment, then grabbed a bottle of water and bundled themselves into the seclusion of the shack.

"Don't use all of it," Dad shouted to them. "Just a couple of dabs for washing. It's too precious to waste."

The girls had only been in the shack for a few moments when I realized something was wrong.

I hurried inside, and initially nothing seemed out of

place. The twins were still in their cotton dresses; they hadn't begun to wash yet. The soap bar was still in its plastic wrapping.

"Helen," Emily murmured. She stood transfixed, holding the bottle of water. Freda crouched next to her, gazing down at the floor. Some of the water from the bottle lay in a patch by her feet. She couldn't take her eyes off it. I touched her arm, and she blinked several times.

"Watch," she said. "Do it, Emms. Do it again."

"No, I don't wanna waste any of the water."

"Just a little," Freda said. "Just to show Helen. Put some on me, like before."

Emily poured a few drops of water onto Freda's bare-skinned forearm. The water did not soak her skin. The opposite happened—the droplets ran off Freda's arm without wetting her at all. Her body seemed to be coated in a resisting substance. The water slipped off, leaving her entirely dry.

Both the twins gazed in awe at the damp pool spreading around their ankles. Freda dropped to the floor, wiping her hand there. She dragged her nails against the dampness as if she missed it, as if trying to claw it back.

"To be inside water," Emily said.

"To be at the heart of it," Freda said.

"To touch it."

"To be within the grip of it." Freda said this with sudden venom, and stared at me. "Something's down in the sea. Something's there."

"What?"

"The *Protector*," she said—and suddenly, surprising even herself, she wept. "Can't you hear it?" she asked. She wiped the tears away, then twisted her wet fingers this way and that, fascinated by the feel of them. "Can't you hear, Helen? It's calling uz. It aches. Oh, it's been waiting so long down there. All alone, forgotten in the deep."

"Waves and no warmth," Emily said, "rest wivout sleep."

I opened out my mind, but there was nothing. Whatever was calling, did so only to the twins.

"The Protector," Freda whispered again.

"Oh, Helen." Emily seized my arm. "It's down there, but we can't reach it with our too-tender bodies. It's too deep under the ocean for uz to go. How can we reach it if it's so far?"

"What is it?" I asked.

She shook her head. "Dunno, but it's alive. It's a real thing," she murmured, clinging to Freda. "It's an old thing."

The twins were full of restless excitement that evening. They were too keyed-up even to eat, and only did so when Walter stood over them and virtually spooned the food down their throats. Following that, they went to bed early and were soon both fast asleep, dreaming of a cold sea.

Deciding not to disturb them, Dad, Walter, and I stayed outside the shack, talking quietly about the events of the day. With no indication in Jenny's mind about what might be next, we agreed to let Emily and Freda make the next move.

"Time for bed ourselves," Dad said a little later and, while Walter went back to his own hut, we crept inside the shack as quietly as we could. Dad couldn't help banging the ceiling as he took off his jacket, but the twins didn't wake.

"I'll stay up and keep an eye on them," he said. "You get some sleep, Helen. You need it."

"I don't think I can, Dad."

"Try, at least."

I did, but sleep wouldn't come, and Dad recognized the pattern of my breathing well enough to tell.

"How are the twins doing?" he asked after a while. "I've been watching them. They seem peaceful enough. Hardly moving. Sleeping like babies."

"They're not, though," I said.

"Really?"

"Strange dreams."

"Everyone's having those, Helen."

"Not ones like these, Dad."

That night, after midnight, rain fell on Coldharbour.

It pelted on our roof, and uproar broke out all around the shack as children tried to find cover.

I jumped out of bed, thinking, Milo? Pushing the shack door open, I stared up, terrified for a second that he wouldn't be there. He was. Of course he was. He hadn't left us.

But I noticed a change: one of Milo's wings was dipped unusually close to the ground.

"What's wrong with him?" Dad asked.

"Nothing," I said. "He's doing it deliberately."

The rain flowed down Milo's wing. The contours of the wing channeled it towards a single Coldharbour location—the small patch around our shack.

"It's only falling on us," Dad gasped.

"No," I said. "It's not meant for us."

"Who then?"

"The twins."

With the first slap of water on the roof Emily and Freda had scampered from the shack. Once they were outside, they couldn't get enough of the rain. They jumped up for it. Emily put out her hands and whooped. Freda poked out her tongue, attempting to capture each drop. The water bounced like sparks off their faces.

After a few minutes Milo repositioned his wing and the downpour came to an end. We were all soaked through, but the twins were dry. Shrugging off their disappointment that the rainfall was over, they kissed each other—and turned to Walter.

"Take uz there," Emily said. "Walts, take uz."

There was no arguing with the look she gave him.

"W-where?" he asked.

"The sea, Walts. As fast as you can."

For once Walter ignored the usual children clutching at him, picking me, the twins and Jenny up. Dad grabbed onto his arm—and Walter ran.

"Hurry, Walts!" Freda pleaded, and he did, dodging between people, taking huge strides across the Milo-illuminated landscape. As we neared the sea, I saw that Coldharbour's entire coastline was packed with children. But Walter wasn't known in this area and the sight of his giant frame made them scatter, giving us an empty stretch of beach to aim for. Three further strides and a single enormous leap took Walter over the heads of the last of the children and into the water. He landed knee-deep, and we all sucked in air, shocked by the sudden coldness.

For a moment it was quiet. The only sounds were the shrieks of some high-flying gulls and the lap of the surf against Walter's thighs.

We all waited. I half-expected to see the ancient creature Emily had mentioned, the one she called the Protector, come crawling and flopping like some nearly-dead thing out of the sea. The twins were enthralled by the sight of the water. They could not take their eyes off it. But they did not try to leave Walter's arms. Instead, they held onto him. I realized what was wrong.

"You can't swim, can you?"

"We was never shown how!" Freda wailed. "Emms never liked the water, and I didn't want to go in, not if she didn't. . . ."

"We gotta do it," Emily said, pinching herself. She

made herself creep down Walter's knee. When her toes met the water she pulled back, cringing. "No, got to," she shrieked, creeping down again. She glanced helplessly at Freda. "I'll do it," she said. "I'll do it, if you will."

"I will, Emms."

Walter said, "Hold on t-to me."

"If I'd a boat," Freda muttered encouragingly in Emily's ear, "I'd sail away."

"If I'd a boat, I'd—" Emily dropped her gaze, too nervous to think up a finish to the rhyme. "C'mon," she said, her teeth chattering. "Walts, take uz in closer to shore, where it's not so bad."

Walter waded into shallower water, where the girls could pull up their dresses and the waves only reached their shins.

"It's cold," Emily muttered. "It's too flipping cold."

"I know," said Freda. "Never mind. It's colder where we're going."

Without letting go of Walter, they asked him to move out a little further. Every few steps he paused, and they lowered their bodies slightly more boldly into the sea. Emily stopped when the water reached her shoulders. She refused to go any further. A wave sloshed into her open mouth, and she choked on it.

"Tastes disgusting!" she screamed.

"It's okay," Freda said, quickly dropping beside her.

"Don't b-be scared!" Walter boomed. "I won't let g-go of you."

Emily rested her cheek against his hand for a moment. "I know you won't. Though you'll 'ave to," she added wistfully. Then, shaking, and still holding onto him, she let out a little scream and submerged her whole body under the waves. So did Freda. Their faces bobbed up moments later, their fingers clutching greedily at Walter.

"We'll be all right, Emms," Freda murmured. "We gotta go down to it. We can't stay 'ere."

"I know," Emily said bleakly. "I know. C'mon then."

Both girls' hands sleepwalked down Walter's body. They slid down the length of his arms until they only held onto his hands. Then his fingers. Then one finger.

They let go.

Panic followed, spluttering and scrambling as their arms beat the water.

"Not yet!" I said, when Walter went to fish them out.

"B-but, Helen, they—"

"Walter, not yet!"

Emily attempted to keep her nose and lips above the water. She panted, her breath coming in sharp gasps. Freda found it slightly easier, pointing her chin stiffly up at the sky. Her arms made choppy waves. Then she relaxed, and her arms struck out more confidently under the water.

"See? Like this, Emms," she said—but Emily was already doing it.

Freda giggled. Emily splashed her, amazed at herself. Both girls swam swiftly and with ease back and forth along the beach shallows. When they returned to us, their minds were made up.

Freda gazed solemnly at her sister.

"Are yer ready?"

"No," she said. "But I'll do it if you'll hold on to me."

"You know I will."

They peered up at Walter and gave him a terrific smile.

"It's all right," Freda told him. "It's all right, now, Walts. We're ready. We are."

"W-w-where are you going?" Walter said, suddenly afraid of losing them.

"There's something down there," Freda said, stroking his hair. "Something wonderful. Come 'ere." Both girls raised their faces to kiss him.

Then they smiled for all of us, and turned outward, towards the open sea. They weren't quite prepared to leave yet, though. For a few minutes they trod water and took deep breaths, readying themselves. Finally, with a last agonized glance at all of us, and causing barely a ripple, they slipped under the waves. The last thing I saw was Emily's hard, chipped toenails flicking beneath the surf.

We waited for them to return. We waited for over two hours. Dawn came, and still there was no sign of them. We waited through sunrise and into the morning. By midday Dad thought we should go back to the shack, but Walter wouldn't budge. He insisted on remaining in exactly the spot the twins had left us. So, while Dad and I stayed on the beach, Walter stood out in the water, with Jenny clinging to his neck, the two of them staring disconsolately out across the gray waves.

"Come here," I whispered to Dad, feeling lonelier and lonelier as the afternoon drew on.

He shuffled up the beach to lie near me. "What's the matter?"

"Nothing. Put your arms around me, that's all. No, closer," I said, wanting it the same way as when I was much younger. He did so, and I thought I might sleep, but the nightmares of children hadn't become fewer, and now there was Walter keeping me awake as well. He never stopped scanning the waves.

Sheer exhaustion meant that I did fall asleep at last, but even then I found no peace because in my dreams there was nothing, nothing, nothing except the Roar.

FIVE

devourer of worlds

THE ROAR

The Roar passed between the stars.

Once, sleek and full-fed, few planets had been large enough to contain the extent of her massive body. That was the period of her best killing weight, a time when she had been dominant even amongst her own kind—a spectacular assassin within a team of assassins.

But that was long ago. Now she was starving. No food in the emptinesses of space. Nothing here in the cold reaches to satisfy her appetite. Only dust. A terrible need made her inhale even this lifeless stuff. Well, she would coat her many stomachs with dust, if that's what she must do to stay alive until she reached the children.

In her weakened state she would never have smelled them at all, except that there were so many. A world full of food! Enough to slake her own hunger and that of the budding killers swarming about inside her flesh—her newborn.

Nearly there now, she told them.

How long had she been on the move? No way to be certain: a crowd of centuries at least. To reduce the pains of hunger on the voyage, she had leaked fluid into her vast stomachs. But she could not quench the great fires that simmered inside them entirely and, with nothing to feed on, they had slowly burned and burned her.

She endured that. For ages she did not roar. She was careful. She moved silently between the galaxies, letting the noisy children guide her. It was so easy to follow them: their chatter never ceased; their minds sprayed in all directions. Good. It meant the Protector she had imprisoned on their world ages before was still too frail to help them. She expected that. The Protector was probably dead. After all, it had been a young one and she had hurt it badly. She had hurt it and concealed it in a place where nothing could hear its silver cries.

From time to time on the journey, the Roar stopped to gnaw on the edges of a dead world or moon. She had no choice. Her teeth were always developing; if she did not use them, the upward-pointing lower set would grow and grow until they curled around and bit into her own face.

To prevent starvation along the way, the Roar had shut down the parts of her body not required for survival: the digestion glands, her speed-musculature, seven of her hearts, forty of her lungs, her clench-limbs and the varied poisons that defined her as the impressive killer she was. Eventually, when her hunger was beyond enduring, she had been forced to turn her massive head and eat her own tail-flukes and lower limbs. When she could eat no more of herself without risking her life, she finally closed off the flow of blood to all inessential organs, including her eyes. It had been a pity to do so, but it did not matter.

Her newborn would be her eyes now.

She kept her once plentiful supply of newborn alive for as long as she could. Finally she had no choice; to avoid her own famishment she ate all except the two strongest.

The two surviving newborn nestled under her skin, sucking her blood into their tiny stomachs. Every suck of them was unending pain, but the Roar endured it, as she had endured everything else. Now, however, she was concerned about what they were doing. The newborn mouths were deep within her body, dangerously close to her main heart. If they started eating that she would never reach the world of the children. The newborn understood that, too—but it had been so long since they fed properly that the Roar knew they might chew the edges of her heart out of sheer desperation.

To keep them occupied for the last part of the journey, she ejected a thin layer of dead skin. Both newborn emerged to bite it, spitting out the driest husks and racing over her back. At least the fragment of skin gave them an object to play with. Without the prospect of a kill, the newborn were terminally bored. Often they ripped at her flesh or at each other, just for something to do.

"Almost there," she told them again.

They had long ago stopped believing her.

"When will we feed?" they demanded.

"Soon."

Scurrying under her belly, pretending her words were true, the strongest of them feebly roared.

She did not answer it. Fear of detection by the Protectors kept her quiet. It had been so long since she properly roared. She longed to do so again. Soon, she thought. Soon. When the children were close enough. When they were close enough to smell individually. When they came close enough to quicken her taste ducts and pitch open her eyes, then she would reinflate her lungs and roar with all her old frenzy.

Caution first, though. To test the preparedness of the world ahead, she initiated a low-intensity diminished howl. At first there had been no reaction from the children. But as she drew closer they had begun to notice: first one child, then six—and now they all heard.

So, the children would have some warning of her arrival.

The young Protector also knew she was coming. The Roar thought she had left it injured beyond repair on their world, but as she neared the Earth she realized that the Protector was not quite dead. It clung weakly to some kind of life. Nevertheless, it remained imprisoned. It had not escaped the bonds she had forged for it in the ocean deeps. Otherwise why would it be calling the children down to it? A Protector reliant for its rescue on such infinitesimally small beings would not be able to assist them. It would also be easy to kill when she arrived.

Hearing these thoughts, the Roar's newborn glowed with renewed confidence. Bursting across her skin, both of them looked out eagerly in the direction they were heading, and for the first time in more than a thousand years they prepared their little stomachs, stirring the embers.

drills

THOMAS

The night passed uneasily for me and the Unearthers.

In the morning there were no obvious additional changes to their bodies, but there was a pressing new problem: food. Without proper hands what were they supposed to do? They'd hardly eaten a thing since they lost their fingers.

Tanni sent a number of the Unearthers out to investigate the food drop-off points we'd heard were springing up inside the Barrier. They returned hours later, awkwardly balancing bags, packets, containers, and other stuff in their arms. Even simple actions, like holding a bottle of water, were impossible for the Unearthers now. So they improvised, wedging the bottles between their wrists and twisting off the tops with their teeth. Eating proved even trickier. The Unearthers had to balance food on their knees and bend down for it. Not easy when your neck is metal-hard.

Tanni saw the opportunity to lighten the atmosphere by getting the youngsters to figure out how to open a packet of chips. It should have been tragic to watch, but it was actually hilarious. The attempts went on for over an hour, delicate little bags of chips exploding all over the place. And just when I thought the Unearthers would never get it right, and the whole game would end miserably, one boy gently squeezed the bottom of a bag, pushing the air up with his palms, while his friend stabbed the top. The first time they tried it the chips spilled everywhere, but pretty soon the two of them were expert little packet-openers—and showing the others.

That stupid chip game. It was only afterwards I realized what a brilliant idea it was of Tanni's. It did far more than develop the Unearthers' handling skills. It forced them to work together as well, kept them occupied and made them share things. And some of the Unearthers actually had a bit of fun! During the game a few couldn't stop laughing, and it wasn't because chips had suddenly become outrageously funny. It was all the pent-up fear, all that dread in them busting to escape. The Unearthers needed to laugh more than they needed to eat. Tanni knew that. He knew how close to breaking point some of them were.

But they obviously couldn't go on like this for long, and I offered Tanni my help. "I can get some of the food ready," I told him. "At least open things for you. It's ridiculous everyone spilling half of it in the mud."

"No," Tanni replied. "I doubt we're getting our hands back, Thomas. We'd better get used to coping without them. I don't want us relying on anyone else."

"At least allow people to help you," I protested. "Why won't you do that? I've seen the way you keep other children away."

"No," Tanni said firmly. "No charity."

"What's the matter with you? It's not charity! People could come in here and do all sorts. Dig your beds, get food prepared, help you dress . . ."

"Yeah, I know they could." Tanni grinned mirthlessly. "And they could hold our drinks of water, and wipe us down when we spill it, and pull our pants down as well when we need them to. . . ."

"Okay, it's embarrassing," I said, "but so what? You *need* help. I don't understand why you're being so stubborn about this."

Making sure the others didn't hear, Tanni said in an undertone, "Here's why. If children trot in here getting us things, doing things for us, how long do you think it'll be before we start to think of ourselves as invalids?"

"That's just stupid," I said.

"Is it? I don't think so. We've got to learn to do things for ourselves. You said it yourself: if we're the second defenders, everything is going to depend on how we face up to the Roar. We've got to be ready for that. All this dealing with food and cleaning up—it's tricky, but we can handle it ourselves. What we can't afford is any sympathy,

Thomas. As soon as we begin to feel sorry for ourselves we're lost."

Tanni was probably right, but it was a lonely path he was taking the Unearthers down. At least a third of them were less than ten years old; a quarter of them were less than five. All of them missed their families.

Tanni didn't want them standing around doing nothing, so he kept them occupied, urging the youngsters to experiment with their new hands. It wasn't apparent how the drill-like parts worked, so they tried everything: slicing into the mud, scooping out great clods of earth, or scraping away at various rocks. Some of the bigger boys applied brute force. They found a boulder and hacked away at it so hard that sparks shot from their hands. Nothing worked, though. Whatever they tried, the Unearthers could never make much of an impression. They did manage to dig a short way down into Coldharbour's muck, but the clingy soil stuck in their drill-parts and they soon got bogged down.

After lunch the enthusiasm of the older Unearthers waned, but Tanni didn't miss a beat. He formed the youngsters into special digging teams. I'd noticed before how good Tanni was with the smaller kids, and it was touching to see them respond. They kept working away for him throughout the heat of the afternoon, their drill-hands lowered proudly.

Eventually, though, even their cooperation lapsed, and Tanni had to call a rest. Late afternoon crept up on us. By the evening, with still no progress being made, all the Unearthers were camped down in the mud, looking tired and defeated.

"We can't go on like this," Tanni whispered to me. "Isn't there more you can do to hurry these changes along? Your beauty's taken us this far. Why won't it complete what it started? We have to be able to dig!"

"How do you know that?" I asked. "Your hands might be for something else."

"No, they're definitely for digging," Tanni said. He licked his lips nervously. "We've been getting messages."

"Oh?"

"Not words. More like information. About rock formations. All of us are getting the same information at the same time. It's as if we're being taught drilling techniques, as if our brains are being programmed for what they need. I was talking to Parminder about it earlier. It scares her, but personally I don't think it's any scarier than what's been happening to our hands." He stared at me. "We just have to keep calm, trust your beauty and let it do its work."

I had no idea what to reply to this unexpected news, but Tanni was right about one thing: my beauty continued to fuel the changes in the Unearthers. It poured into them at the same ferocious pace Milo had required only in his final needy hours.

"Whatever you do, don't hold back," Tanni said.

"I'm not," I told him. "I'm giving you everything I've got."

He placed a heavy drill-hand on my shoulder. "Sorry," he murmured. "I know you are. Given how many of the Unearthers there are, it's amazing what your beauty's already managed to do. It's just . . ."

"I know," I said. "The longer this goes on, the harder it is to keep everyone from completely freaking out."

"Exactly. Especially given the new changes."

By that he meant how much bigger the Unearthers were getting. It had started during the afternoon with their wrists, and I suppose none of us should have been surprised—their normal wrists had always seemed too frail for their drill-hands. Throughout the day the wrists thickened. The thickening was followed by a broadening of their arms and shoulders. By dusk even the weakest of the boys and girls had upper bodies as powerful as a muscular man's.

The revolt against Tanni's leadership started brewing before sunset. Parminder led it; she and several other teenagers had put up with everything else, but they couldn't accept this latest outrage to their bodies. I warned Tanni about their hushed conversations.

"I know," he said. "I've heard them. Let them talk. Let it come to a head. In the end they've got to make their own minds up about what they're going to do."

The number of Unearthers listening to Parminder grew throughout the night. Eventually, when she felt she had enough support on her side to confront Tanni, she marched over to us. She stood there, the size of a small bull, glaring at me. Her shoulder muscles bulged under her dress.

In one hand she held a small jagged rock. It was her favorite stone. I'd seen her dreamily brushing it against her face, the first morning I met the Unearthers.

"Look!" she yelled. "See this rock! I'm still holding it! I can't stop stroking this ridiculous rock!" She trembled, throwing it down. "And see my arm? My dad's built like a brick house, but even he doesn't have an arm this big!" She glared at me. "What are you doing to us?"

I didn't blame her for being angry. I wanted to reassure her, but how? I couldn't even promise her things would improve.

"I've made up my mind," she said. "I'm not staying here any more. I don't care what Tanni says. Check out these shoulder muscles! I've become Arnie flaming Schwarzenegger in less than a day! My friends are all like the Incredible Hulk!"

A boy half laughed, but Parminder cut him off angrily.

"Look at all of us!" She raised her arms as if they belonged to some monster. "Tanni keeps saying we've got to dig, and we keep getting these thoughts rammed into our heads about digging, digging. But how? With these weird hands? It's crazy! We've tried everything. Shovels would be quicker! My old granddad could dig faster than us! I know," she said, her voice rising hysterically, "maybe we're supposed to head-butt our way down? We haven't tried that yet, have we?" Parminder glared defiantly at

Tanni. She couldn't wait for him to react. She looked as if she wanted to hit him. Tanni gave her a grim smile.

"Do you think this is funny?" Parminder screamed at him. "Is that what you think? Is it fun for you? A game?"

"No, of course not," Tanni said, standing up to face her. "Nothing's remotely funny about any of it. I feel just the same as you. Do you think I don't want my old body back? I'm scared as well! I'd love to pretend none of this is happening, but we can't, can we? If we do, who's going to defend Coldharbour when the Roar arrives?"

Parminder hesitated. "We're not the only ones who can do that. There are hundreds of thousands of others here, and—"

"No," Tanni said firmly. "There might be hundreds of thousands of children in Coldharbour, but there aren't thousands of Unearthers. If there were they'd have joined us, or we'd at least have heard of them by now. I don't like being picked out for this any more than you do, Parminder, but let's not pretend other kids out there are going to save our skins from the Roar, because they're not."

Parminder stared furiously at him. "There's Milo!"

"Ah yes. Milo. I thought you might mention that. Milo, Milo, Milo. Well, take a good long look at him. Go on!" Tanni said, raising his voice to address them all. "And while you're doing it think about all the changes Thomas told us Milo had to go through. Climbing over rubbish dumps with his hands falling off, in all that pain as well. Milo did most of it on his own, too. It's a good job Milo didn't give up, eh? I suppose he could have done. When his wings appeared, he could have flown off. He must have been tempted. He must have been scared. I'll bet he's scared now. But where is he? Right up there, that's where! Over us! Protecting us! We take it for granted that he'll just stay up there, don't we? You hear people saying that all the time—Milo, he'll look after us, the first defender against the Roar. But you know something: they don't have to face it. Milo *knows* he's the first defender. He really is!"

"But look at us!" Parminder retorted, tearing at her dress. "Look at me! I'm disgusting: hard, swelling up! At least Milo still looks human!"

"I'm still human," Tanni said. "At least I think so. And so are you. All of us are. Aren't we still human, even if we haven't got any fingers?"

"I can't stand it!" Parminder snapped. "I won't!"

Tanni considered that a moment, and then turned to the rest of the Unearthers.

"Did any of you actually think that swollen knuckles were going to be enough? Did you? Honestly? How could they be enough to fight against the Roar?" He shook his head. "Listen to me, or don't listen to me, whatever you want. But the Roar's coming. You know that. You've all heard *that* voice. Compared to the creature making it, the differences between us and other children are nothing."

"But what's next?" a boy called out.

"I don't know," Tanni said. "And I'm not going to

pretend everything's going to be okay from now on, either. It's not going to be okay. We're probably going to change even more. These changes to our muscles . . . they're hideous, but I think our bodies need to be stronger to be able to dig . . ."

"I'm going," Parminder said. "I've heard enough. I'm leaving. I don't care what you say. And I'm not the only one."

"All right," Tanni replied. "I won't try to stop you. But if we all give in, remember what that means. It means we're leaving Milo on his own against the Roar."

Tanni said nothing after that, letting them make up their own minds.

I'd like to say that Parminder reconsidered and agreed to stay, but Tanni's plea didn't change her mind. Twenty-three more Unearthers left with her, but the rest remained, and there was no more complaining as they prepared their sleep-holes later that night. When I spoke to Tanni in the early hours of the morning, I expected him to be elated, but he wasn't.

"We need them all," he said to me. "And we need Parminder more than most. She's good with the girls, much better than me. I wish I could have persuaded her to stay. I'd give anything to have them all back."

For a while Tanni sat gloomily on his own. Then he went off to make sure the youngest Unearthers were bedding down properly. He didn't need to. Each of them had dug their hole to a good depth, without needing to be nagged. Within an hour many were asleep, or wishing they were. Tanni returned to me, his shoulders even more massive than they had been earlier. He looked like a tank.

"Do something different," I said.

"Eh?"

"I've been thinking. What's the one thing you haven't tried? What did you stop everyone from doing right from the beginning?"

"I'm not following you, Thomas."

"You made them dig holes to sleep in. You stopped them from approaching each other."

"There wasn't any choice. They'd have cut themselves to pieces."

"Would they? Maybe. I'm not sure anymore. Take a gamble."

"Ask some of them to sleep together out in the open, you mean?"

"Yes."

"What do you think'll happen?"

"I don't know," I said. "Probably nothing. Maybe they will cut each other. We'll have to watch carefully."

Tanni stared at me for a moment. Then he woke up four of the youngsters he knew best. All had been sleeping, and only blearily followed what he was asking of them, but they agreed to stay on the surface near one another. Tanni kept a close eye on them while they drifted back to sleep. After an hour they'd moved slightly towards each other, nothing more. A chillier wind than usual was dragging in over the sea. Seeing them exposed to it, I began to regret what I was putting them through.

"No, it's okay," Tanni said. "They're not waking up, so they can't be too cold, and Milo will do something about it if the wind gets too strong anyway. Let them stay like this a while longer. You go to sleep. I'll keep watch for a while."

I nodded, pulled my jacket up around my neck and surprised myself by falling into a light doze almost immediately. A sharp cry woke me. I leapt up, thinking that perhaps Tanni had fallen asleep himself and one of the Unearthers had been injured.

I was wrong. An argument had broken out between two of the children he'd chosen.

"Get off," one was saying.

"You get off. You started it. Get your hand away from me."

"I can't."

"What?"

"I can't! It's stuck!" The boy wrenched his arm, but could not separate himself from the other's hand.

Tanni knelt beside them.

"It's okay," he said. "Calm down. Let me see."

Both boys brought their hands up together; being joined, they had no choice. And this is what we saw: the knuckle-blades along the edge of one boy's hand filled the other's. The mesh of their hands was perfect. No matter how hard they tugged, they could not disengage themselves.

The rest of the Unearthers were soon awake. The two joined boys were frightened, and didn't particularly like being the center of attention, but Tanni stayed nearby, reassuring them. A few minutes later we heard familiar voices approaching—Parminder and the others who'd left. A boy and girl amongst them also had joined hands.

Parminder tramped towards us. "We've come back . . . only to know what this means," she said testily.

"Show me your hand," Tanni said to her.

"What? Why should I?"

"You'll see."

Frowning, she held out a hand. "No," Tanni said, studying it. "Your other hand. Your right hand."

She did so. Tanni overlaid his own left hand against it, drill against drill. There was a distinct sequence of clicks.

Parminder looked at him blankly.

"Don't you see?" Tanni said. "I should have realized this much earlier. The differences in our knuckles, the kinks to right or left . . . look at the crisscross formation of the ridges. They're drills, sure enough, but they don't work alone. They need a partner."

Parminder blinked at him. "What? I'm your partner?"

Tanni grinned. "I'm afraid so."

Everyone gathered around them.

"Hey!" Parminder complained, as Tanni dragged her arm to the ground.

"Sorry," he said. "Just had an idea." He lowered his left arm. She nervously bent down with him until both their hands, like two joined circles, were flat against the soil.

"What now?" Parminder asked.

"Now press," Tanni said.

Ever so gently Parminder put pressure on the palm of her hand.

Instantly there was an eruption of sound—the drill bits turning like rotors. Tanni and Parminder jumped in surprise as the ground exploded under them. Within seconds they were buried halfway up the arm. Gasping, they lifted their hands.

The drills shut down at once.

Tanni stared at the rest of the Unearthers in triumph.

"This is it!" he said. "Twin up! Everyone twin up! Check for opposing shaped hands, for hands with drill parts that turn in the opposite direction from your own." He nudged my jacket and laughed. "That's how we're meant to dig, Thomas! All along, *this* was how we were meant to do it!"

Within minutes the hand comparisons were made and pairs formed. After that, the Unearthers couldn't wait to begin. They didn't discuss what approach they would take. They just started drilling. That was all they wanted to do now.

Tanni gave the nod for the two boys who'd joined first to lead the way. They leaned against their drill-hands and pushed. Within minutes the hole they'd made was so deep we could barely see them. Their broad backs toiled on and their faces never looked up. All around the other Unearthers established their own holes. Mud blasted everywhere, threatening to bury me. I moved aside, standing clear.

Tanni and Parminder were the last to leave. "Well, partner?" Tanni said, smiling away at her. There was a new gleam in Parminder's eye. "I'll lead," she said. Tanni nodded, winked at me, and lowered his arm.

"Wait," I said, a dozen questions rushing into my mind—but Tanni and Parminder had already disappeared into the soil.

I gazed around. A series of almost perfectly round holes punctured the flatness of Coldharbour. I peered over the lip of one, wondering what I was supposed to do now. For some reason, I felt good. I'm not sure why. I think it was because although I had no idea where the Unearthers were heading, my beauty seemed sure. Its authority, its strength, reached out from me, following them down their holes.

All night the sound of drilling raged. Not for a moment did it stop.

SEVEN

celebration

HELEN

We waited for the twins to return from the sea. All that day we waited, and on through the night, and just before dawn next morning, when Dad had lost hope, and I thought Walter would go out of his mind from gazing for so long at the incoming waves, the twins' heads popped back up.

First Freda's upturned nose; then Emily, coughing her lungs out.

I'd half-expected the twins to be carrying some ancient wonder between them out of those waters, but they were alone. Walter splashed out to pick them up, and Emily flopped into his arms, wildly opening and closing her mouth, needing to speak. "Shush," Walter said, but she shook her head.

"The Protector's too far!" she wailed. "We couldn't . . . we couldn't . . . reach it! Oh, Walts, and even if we could, it's too big for just our 'ands to pick its precious bones free."

Reading their minds, I knew that the twins had swum through near-frozen seas in absolute darkness to find the Protector. They'd gone almost to the bottom of the world, but it still wasn't enough: the Protector remained beyond their reach. Only once, at the end of their voyage, had they glimpsed it—a creature that stretched across the floor of an ocean, heaving against its bonds.

Emily and Freda didn't speak on the way back to the shack. They merely tucked themselves into Walter, clutching at him for every scrap of warmth they could find. Neither girl wanted to talk about what had happened during their time under the waves, but they didn't have to. I knew the truth: the twins had almost died out there. Only Freda, holding on desperately herself at the end, had kept Emily alive during the final miles up to the surface.

When we got back, Dad dealt with the questions of children around us as best he could while Walter carried the exhausted twins inside the shack. They crept onto their mattress like old ladies. I borrowed extra blankets, but the twins couldn't get warm. All day they lay twisting on their bed, haunted by their failure to reach the Protector.

Jenny was distraught about the state of Emily. "Ah, none of it's your fault, Jens," Emily managed to whisper in her ear. "Why would yer think that?"

I looked in Jenny's mind, and realized that she had no

idea what was next. She'd made herself a mud seagull, but she only seemed to want the bird as a simple plaything to replace Agatha.

As for the twins, they remained restless. Despite what had happened, they were anxious to be back in the sea again, and kept getting up from their mattress. Dad and I tried to stop them, but they wouldn't listen. Freda swayed wonkily to her feet, holding her hands out in front of her in case she fell. Emily couldn't get up at all until much later. When she finally did she looked pitiable, shuffling around the shack on her knees.

"Why ain't we strong enough, Helen?" Freda groaned. "Why ain't we? Why can't we reach it?"

"We 'ave to!" Emily shouted. "I know how we are, but we 'ave to go back!" She hobbled around the shack. "We can't leave it there. How can we?"

"Emily," I said, trying to make her understand, "you can't go back yet. You can't even stand up."

"I can," she said. "I can!" Legs shaking—deliberately ignoring Freda's supporting arm—she pressed her heels into the floor. With a huge effort she held her weight briefly on all four sets of her nails.

"You'll die if you go back there now," I told her.

"You don't know that!" she snapped back defiantly.

But I think she did, and eventually both girls stopped trying to stand and accepted that they had to rest. Later, a small degree of hope crept back into Emily's voice as she made a request from her bed. "Helen," she said. "Walter's birthday's been forgotten. That's not right."

"It doesn't matter," I said. "That's the last thing you should be thinking about. Walter doesn't care. He wants you to rest, and—"

"No, no . . . I *want* to," Emily said, reaching out her hand to me.

Looking at her, I knew she meant it. Even if she could only do it for a while, she wanted to forget about the failure to reach the Protector, and make life more normal again.

"We've talked about it, Helen," Freda said, "and we both want to do it. Please don't stop uz. That boy, ee's always doing stuff for others. And ee suffered while we was gone. You know how much. I think it was almost worse for Walts than for uz. Let uz do this for him."

"All right," I said, seeing how much they both wanted to. "All right. I'll put the word out. Tomorrow then, if you're well enough."

"We will be."

Early next morning the twins were up and about before anyone else, and more their old selves. "Keep Walts busy and not watching uz while we organize things," Freda told me.

To do that, Dad had the idea of setting up an exercise class, and Jenny whipped up so much enthusiasm from the smallest kids that Walter led them with a few half-hearted jumping jacks and leg stretches. All the while he kept an eye on the shack, worried when he couldn't see the twins. I distracted him by getting about ten toddlers to hang like dumbbell weights off his arms. Meanwhile, the twins sneaked off to get the small stash of food that had been concealed in a nearby tent.

Dozens of children had contributed. It wasn't much to speak of, just bread, scraps of meat, vegetables, and a few sandwiches they'd managed to find at the drop-off points, but it was still the biggest selection of food I'd seen in one place in Coldharbour. All our bellies had shrunk somewhat since we'd been here, but Walter's extra size meant that he was constantly hungry—though he never complained.

The twins were restless to get the celebration under way, but there was a hitch. Someone must have accidentally let on at the last minute, and our birthday boy had camped himself in embarrassment firmly inside his hut. He wouldn't leave it, no matter how hard Emily rapped on the wood.

"I'm b-busy," came Walter's muffled voice. "I can't come out now."

"You open that door," Emily said firmly. "There ain't nothing you're up to in there that can't wait."

"I'm . . . busy."

"Doing what?"

". . . P-planning things." It was all he could think to say.

Freda winked at Jenny. "I knew something like this'd

happen. I think you know what to do, dear."

Jenny smiled, opened her mouth—and screamed.

The hut door sprang open and Walter had her pinned against his chest in a second. There were scores of children outside, all of them laughing and suddenly starting up with "Happy Birthday." Walter gave Jenny a scowl. Then he saw the food, and you should have seen his eyes light up. But it never even occurred to him to eat it himself. Before the twins could stop him, he was handing out bits of sandwiches and slices of bread all around. Most of the food went down throats in seconds, but the twins had kept a certain amount behind.

"This is just for you," Emily said, folding her arms. "We'll see you full for once!"

Walter frowned, attempting to outmaneuver them. "But I'm not . . . n-not hungry!" he said.

"Yeah, right," Freda muttered.

Grabbing a handful of ham, she scampered up his body and tried shoving it directly in his mouth. At first Walter refused, keeping his lips tight shut, but the twins were having none of it. Emily tickled him until he had to open his mouth, then Freda pushed the ham down. One gulp and it disappeared. Another, and a meat pudding was gone. Walter kept trying to prevent them, but the twins were tickling his armpits, and Jenny was working on his chest, until he held up his hands in surrender.

After that, there was no stopping the twins. Emily scrambled up, anchoring herself on his shoulder. "Right, c'mon!" she said in a businesslike way. With one hand she hung onto Walter's neck. With her other she rammed handfuls of food into his mouth that Freda passed up to her. She did it with determination, as if she was stoking up an engine.

Walter kept taking it off her whenever he could and handing it to someone else, but Emily packed a fair amount down him before Walter patted that impressive stomach of his and wiped his lips. "Enough!" he said. "E-nough!"

"No way, Walts!" Freda said. "No way! You got to eat this!"

Someone had been far and wide to find him—a chocolate slice. Chocolate in Coldharbour! Impossible! When Walter insisted on Jenny having it the twins chased him round our shack, trying to shove that hard-won chocolate down his throat. They were merciless, scrambling over his back, pinching his sides, anything to distract him. Finally, Emily poked Walter in his full belly and Freda took the chance to stuff the slice in his mouth.

Walter let out a delighted little moan and sat back.

Jenny crept onto his leg and stretched up to kiss him on the cheek. "Happy birthday, Walter!" she cried. "Happy birthday! Happy birthday!"

And then everyone else was joining in, cheering over and over and shaking Walter's hand and clapping his back. Walter thanked them all vigorously, his grin working overtime. "You certainly have an appetite,

Walter," Dad said.

"I'm s-sorry," Walter apologized. The twins wrapped themselves partway around his belly, as far as their arms could stretch. A bit of carrot slipped down Walter's face.

"If I'd a cloth, I'd wipe 'im down!" Emily said.

"If I'd a hose," Freda said, "I'd splash 'is crown!"

They looked so happy, and I realized that nothing could have distracted them better from their nightmare under the sea than this. And do you know something? Walter knew that, too. He saw the smiles on their faces and he looked at me and he knew.

"Presents!" someone said. "Presents! Presents!"

"Wait a minute." The twins went scurrying off to our shack. Days before they'd collected the necessary materials, and for half the night they'd been secretly working on finishing the gifts. Emily carried one cautiously; Freda carried the other, her eyes gleaming.

Shoes.

Not real shoes, of course. You couldn't find anything to fit Walter's enormous feet. These shoes were homemade. Only the twins would have had the patience to sew dozens of strips of leather together taken from old boots, bags, hats, and who-knows-what-else they'd scavenged from the dumps.

The shoes were works of art. The twins lugged them over to Walter and dropped them beside him. Walter glanced nervously at me. I knew why. The twins had tried endless times in the past weeks to make a pair that would stay on his feet. He didn't want to disappoint them again, especially in their fragile state of mind.

Walter, with the utmost care, placed his big toes into the ends. When nothing went wrong there, he slowly eased in the remainder of his feet.

"A p-perfect fit!" he declared, before they were even halfway on.

They weren't, though. They were slightly too big. Freda and Emily started fussing around him at once, bending the shoes—and Walter's feet—into shape. Then they made him walk around. Walter took a couple of tentative strides. "They're v-very soft," he said. "They're v-very w-warm." He was happy to leave it at that.

Emily smiled tightly.

So did Freda. "Run about," she said.

Walter did—a few tiny jumps on the spot. The shoes did not disintegrate. There were several cheers, but Emily gave the cheerers a murderous glare. She was determined to fully test-drive the shoes. She wouldn't be happy unless Walter ran all the way across Coldharbour in them. Luckily, while Walter showed us all how easily he could twiddle his toes inside, Dad caught on and gave Jenny the signal she was waiting for. She flung her arms wide.

"Bring out the main present!" she announced at the top of her voice.

I knew exactly how long it had taken a group of boys and girls to drag this item from a distant dump. It was a car door. Not the same one Walter had been forced to leave behind in the rain a few days ago—no one could find that, it was probably propping up someone's roof by now—but a newish, sports-car door. It was a curvaceous chrome-yellow, with tinted windows and not a hint of rust anywhere. Many of those in our neighborhood had spent the last hour or so on a final polishing.

I thought Walter was going to die when he saw it. He was speechless. He was so happy that he didn't even want to touch it. He only wanted to look at it. He was too scared to hold it in case he damaged it. "Go on!" Emily reassured him. "It's yours, yer know!" Walter reached out reverentially. He took the door in one hand and stroked it with his fingertips.

Jenny had the final present. In fact, three separate small presents: the mud dolls of the twins, a bit of chocolate she'd been keeping back, and a flower. The flower was slightly worse for wear, but Jenny had brought it from home the day she came into Coldharbour. Walter knew that, too.

"I can't," he said. "N-no, Jenny, that's yours. I c-can't."

"Take it. I want you to."

Seeing how much it meant to her, Walter did. He put it carefully in his jacket pocket.

"Speech," someone said, and soon they were all chanting it. "Speech! Speech! Come on! Speech!"

Walter's face dropped. A speech! He'd never been asked for one of those before. There was plenty of huffing as he made himself ready. Plenty of smiles. He laughed, trying to put himself at ease, but that stutter hadn't given him much mercy in the past and it wasn't about to now.

"I . . ." he started. "I . . ."

We waited.

"I . . . I w-would . . . w-w-w-would . . ."

We waited patiently. The sun rose up the sky.

Walter licked his lips. "I would l-like to thank you all very, very much f-for your . . ."—he readied himself for this last word—"generosity." Some people's mouths fell open. He'd managed to say the sentence virtually in one go. And having done so, Walter swayed a little. He grinned cockily. Everyone cheered like mad.

The final item, the birthday cake, was brought out by Dad. It was a little strawberry cupcake someone had gone all the way to the southern drop-off for. We didn't have any candles—even the twins couldn't find those—but Walter didn't care. Dad presented it to him with panache and Walter, closing his eyes, ate part of it, gave the rest to a girl hanging off his elbow and made a wish. Only I knew what he wished for, and he swore me to secrecy.

Games followed, and the smaller children were still playing them in the middle of the afternoon when Walter said that he needed a rest. Liar. He'd had an idea. He'd been putting it off, but with everyone all together and at ease this seemed like a good time to tell them. When he discussed it quietly with me and Dad we agreed, but neither of us had any idea how his regular day and nighttime visiting children were going to take it. Most of Walter's so-called visitors weren't really visitors anymore. They spent every single waking and sleeping moment with him if they could. And that was the problem, of course. There were too many. There was no way Walter could watch out for all these children when the Roar arrived. Even his broad shoulders couldn't hold them all.

But how to tell them? Walter had agonized over it many times. To the youngest in Coldharbour who'd met him, Walter represented Mum and Dad and something even better all wrapped up in one perfect package.

But this cozy relationship couldn't go on, and Walter was determined to say his piece. He was going to make a proper speech. Walter and speechmaking weren't exactly invented for each other, though, and you could see him shifting inside those new shoes of his. Seeing that he was about to talk the toddlers all stopped what they were doing and blinked up at him adoringly. Walter gazed without hope at me. I nodded, trying to encourage him.

"Well," he began, sucking in some air, "well, what I w-want to say is, to y-you all, this is to you all . . ." He took a breather. "What I'm asking you, n-not all of you, but the ones who c-can't . . . fit in my hand . . ." He held a hand up for all to see, to be certain they understood. They didn't. His hand measurement meant nothing to anyone, because even the biggest children could squeeze into Walter's hand if they had to. "What I'm asking f-f-f-for . . . w-what I'm—"

Dad waded boldly in.

"Now listen," he said, staring down at all the politely upturned faces. "What Walter is telling you is that he's not going to be able to protect you all when the Roar comes." Silence followed that, dead silence. I think Dad had even managed to shock some of the teenagers. "Now don't give me those stares," he said. "You all know it's not possible for Walter to look after everyone." No one nodded in agreement with him except me. "Walter's only one person," he went on more hesitantly. "That means he can only take care of the very youngest children from now on, those who don't have an older brother or sister to watch out for them, or a friend. That's what he wanted to tell you."

Dad's speech wasn't going down too well. Most of the children who normally accompanied Walter had already measured themselves against his hand and found they could fit comfortably. A few—they couldn't help it—had started to cry. Others still didn't know what it all meant. Many were looking sidelong at Walter, and gesturing at Dad as if he was some kind of idiot.

Walter stood there, shoulders bowed. This was killing him. Milo's last words before he went aloft into the sky had been "Walter! Protect them all!"—and Walter took that literally. No matter how many times the twins, Dad, or I had talked to him about it over the past days, Walter took that to mean not only us but everyone in Coldharbour.

He spent the rest of the day taking individual children aside to explain what he meant and why he had to do it. Even then some wouldn't accept it, and I didn't blame them. We all wanted our own personal Walter when the Roar came. These young children weren't stupid; it was only Walter they had any true faith in.

That night was the last one most of his visitors spent with him. He allowed them that, one last night. They all stayed outside with him; no one went into the hut, and the car door was left in the mud, forgotten. Jenny joined Walter, too, sleeping in the crook of his arm as she did every night, her hand curling and uncurling in his hair. Walter thought Jenny understood, but she didn't. She never for one second believed that Walter's words applied to her. The next morning—when Walter settled down to deciding how many children he could safely look after— Jenny joined him, helping them to form a neat line. "You're too big," she said to one boy, sending him away.

Actually, Jenny was always meant to be the exception. Walter intended to keep her close no matter what happened. But he didn't want to let the example of her overshadow what he'd said too quickly to the other children. He tried to explain all this to her, but she took it the wrong way. That night, when he asked her to join me and Dad in the shack with the twins, she couldn't believe it. She blinked at him, and there were tears.

"Milo said you have to take care of me," she argued, when he wouldn't change his mind. When that didn't work, she demanded all three of her presents back. She took them off him, threw them down, kicked his car door and swung on her heel, stomping over to our shack. She didn't say a word as she entered. The twins let her cuddle down next to them.

It was an emotional, unhappy night for Jenny. And it was an unhappy night for Walter, too; he knew how distraught she was, and so many of his regular visitors were gone.

In the early hours Jenny got up to use the latrine outside, and I listened in afterwards as she started up a conversation. She was chatting to a group of children. They were about Jenny's size and age, and all of them missed Walter bitterly. Jenny was direct with them. She told them that the only reason she wasn't with Walter right now was *not* because Walter had rejected her, but because she wanted it that way. She had *asked* him to let her go to the shack. Walter needed his peace, she said. We all had to grow up. It was about time some of the more stupid and selfish little kids realized that around here.

She marched back inside and I motioned for her to lie beside me for the rest of the night. "I'm fine," she said, before I could say a thing.

That night Jenny muttered out loud once or twice in her sleep, and it was Walter's name on her lips. But in her dreams there was another name being called. I was surprised, because the name wasn't that of Walter, or even that of her brother, Milo. The name, over and over, was Thomas.

EIGHT

the smile

THOMAS

I stood in the mud between the holes of the Unearthers, listening.

For over ten hours they'd gone at it. Ten hours of nonstop drilling. It was mid-morning before they returned to the surface. Even then it was only Tanni and Parminder. I heard the percussive impact of their drills hammering upward through the soil.

Tanni's head emerged first, and I found myself running towards him. I'd missed Tanni in the night, but I had no idea how much until I saw his metal head grinning out of that hole. Parminder spat dust from her mouth, cursing the light, but she too was grinning.

Tanni raised their drill-hands in triumph.

"Get over here, Thomas!" he hollered. "Wait till you see what we've been doing!" He blew some earth off Parminder's face. "You'll scare Thomas to death, the way you look," he said to her, laughing.

"No way I'm as ugly as you," she shot back.

Parminder and Tanni cracking jokes! I'd never expected those two personalities to become friends so soon, but why not? Weren't we all in this together? Of course we were.

Their bodies were a shock, though. More changes had occurred overnight. It was their eyes I noticed first: there was definitely an extra lid, a covering; you saw it when they blinked. I tried not to show any surprise—it must have been hard enough for them to deal with—but Tanni saw my expression and shrugged.

"Handsome, eh? Pretty things, me and Parminder." He prodded his nose—or what was left of it, because there wasn't much. It was completely flat, with no nostrils, only thin slits. I couldn't help staring. "I know," Tanni said. "They're weird. But we breathe through them fine, and this way the muck stays out of our lungs during tunneling. Guess how far we've drilled down? Oh, forget it, we'll show you how far."

I peered anxiously over the lip of the hole.

Tanni's eyes shone. "Not scared, are you? Don't worry, I won't let that valuable body of yours get damaged." And with that he scooped me against his hard body, lowered his drill-hand together with Parminder—and we dropped.

We traveled down, with minor slow-ups, for over two minutes.

"Some ride, eh?" Tanni said, but when he felt me cringing against his shirt, he put his arm more securely around my waist. Finally the tunnel flattened out and we came to a sliding halt.

We were in a cave. Tunnel-chutes like the one we'd emerged from punctuated the lower cave walls. Dozens of exits ended up here; others in the floor dropped straight down into the earth.

That's when I realized something—I could see. I could see everything. The cave was lit. The light came from the Unearthers themselves. Their heads glowed. I hadn't noticed on the surface, because the glow was mellow, like reflected bronze.

"Welcome to Base Camp," Tanni said cheerfully, tapping his skull. "These handy new torch-heads show us what we're doing. We carved this place out in less than an hour. What do you think?"

"It's . . ." I didn't know what to say.

"Not home sweet home exactly," Tanni said, "but it'll do. We can rest here more easily than in the cramped tunnels lower down. Check this out for sharpness." He showed me his and Parminder's joined hands. "See, no blunting yet. All this time we've been drilling, but the edges are still perfect. That's your beauty's doing, Thomas. It's been brilliant, reaching right down here to us. And it's done its job. We've been tunneling fine so far. But there's a problem. The drills you've given us are only made of steel. Tempered steel, it's tough as hell, but not tough enough to get through the resistant rock below."

"We're expecting to hit areas of flammable natural gas or poisonous hydrogen sulphide gas," Parminder went on. "Plus we're getting fairly close to hard igneous rock formations. To get through them our drill-parts need to be reinforced with polycrystalline diamond and carbide inserts."

"What?" I said. "Parminder, I haven't got a clue what you're talking about."

"Diamonds are forty to fifty times as hard as steel," she said. "We need diamonds."

"How do you know that? Are you still getting information sent to you?"

"All the time," Tanni said. "And now we know where we're heading, too."

"Where?"

"Deep." He pointed down one of the shafts under us. "Much deeper than anyone's gone before. That's the reason we've been changing so much, Thomas. We've had to."

"But what's down there?"

"We don't know yet. But it's waiting. Waiting to be dug out. To be freed. Whatever it is, it's intelligent, too—and understands what's under us. We only vaguely understand some of the information it's giving us about geology—"

"Hold on," I said. "It's *talking* to you?"

"No, not really." Tanni lowered his face. "Not words. I don't think it's capable of that anymore. It's ill. It's injured. We're only getting . . . stray thoughts between its screams."

I looked at him.

"I know," he murmured. "It's awful. It's locked in the Earth's core, Thomas, and it's *burning down there*. It's on fire. That's why I brought you down here. We need your beauty closer to us. We've just got to develop better drill-hands if we're going to reach whatever it is before the Roar arrives."

There were tears in the corners of Tanni's eyes. I'd never seen those from him before, and although he was slightly embarrassed, I wasn't. There was a real aura of destiny about the Unearthers now. I didn't share their thoughts about whatever was under us, but finally the Unearthers' massive drill-hands, gleaming faces, and hulking bodies all made sense. And I remembered something else. I remembered the time when Milo needed me, and how I'd held back my beauty, appalled by his tube-throat and deformed hands. This time I wouldn't do that.

"I'll give you whatever you need," I said.

Parminder stared at me expectantly. "We need those carbide and diamond inserts."

"I don't know if I can provide them," I said uncertainly. "I mean, I'm here, and I'll go wherever you want. I'm happy to join those Unearthers at the drill-face, if that's where my beauty is needed most. But my beauty's not like a tap. I can't just turn it up a notch. I'm already giving you everything I have."

Parminder was unable to hide her disappointment. Tanni clapped me on the back with his free arm.

"I knew you'd go down into the depths with us," he said. "I told Parminder I wouldn't even have to ask. But it's a lot worse down at the drill-face than you think, Thomas. It's filthy and hot. You're going to sweat. You're going to hate it."

I grinned. "What are we waiting for?"

Tanni grinned back, clasped me to him—and the three of us dropped.

The second camp the Unearthers had established lower down was amazing: a stiflingly hot cave with tunnel off-shoots leading to the distant drill-face. Networks of intricate connecting passageways also linked back to Base Camp and the surface. Three tunnels in the floor had been blocked off.

"Underground water," Tanni explained. "Several of us nearly drowned heading that way. We've got to be careful. But if we're too careful we'll never get anywhere. That's the trouble, striking a balance."

He took me down to the drill-face itself, a sweltering, nearly airless tube filled with dust and toiling Unearther children. "You won't be able to stay down here long," Tanni said. "We're okay, but you'll pass out with the heat."

I watched the drill teams at work. The sound they made in the confined space of the tunnel was deafening, but only for me; the Unearthers had insulating flaps over their ears—another new adaptation.

Once I arrived with my beauty, the lead drillers blasted more effectively through the rock. I stayed with them for as long as I was able, but after only a few suffocating minutes of heat down there I was a wreck. Tanni had to take me back up to Second Camp to cool down. As soon as I could, I returned to the drill-face. The problem was staying down there. I discovered that by remaining absolutely still and breathing only through my nose I could handle the heat better.

I urged my beauty on, but it was a stubborn force. It flowed out the same as before: the same steady lapping into the Unearthers, no more, no less.

I don't know how much time went by. No way to tell if it was day or night even. The hours passed, with Tanni yanking me back and forth between the ever more distant drill-face and Second Camp whenever I was about to pass out.

He'd divided the Unearthers into shifts. A drill-team was composed of four linked pairs. The younger Unearthers generally created the side passages needed to store the loose debris from the main drilling tunnels. The bigger kids did most of the heavy work. Each of them spent thirty minutes maximum at the drill-face, then fresher teams would hoist them out and slide smoothly into position behind.

But progress was slow. Despite the drill-teams working with a dedication that was scary to watch, the layer of rock they were in was brutally hard granite. Rock chips kept flying off the drill-face, hitting them. That's when you saw why they needed those metal bodies; they'd have been killed otherwise. Some of the Unearthers had so many pits, dents, and scratches across their faces that they were scarred almost beyond recognition, but I never saw any of them complain. Where the rock was especially compact steel shutters lowered in place over the Unearthers' eyes, and they drilled blind. Once I heard a muffled explosion in a connecting tunnel. That was the only time I saw the drilling pause. Tanni checked what had taken place, waved it off as nothing, and the drilling resumed.

And then something strange happened, something I wouldn't understand until later. The sound of the Roar ripped through us. No surprises there; even down here I knew it would reach us, and I shuddered as its voice passed by. But here was the odd thing: the Unearthers didn't react. No wincing or flinching from them. No clenching of metal-reinforced teeth. The drilling went on as freely as if nothing had happened at all.

Eventually, after countless trips to the drill-face, my body simply couldn't take any more of the incessant heat, and I lost consciousness. When I awoke again I was too tired to open my eyes, but I recognized the echoey sounds of Second Camp. A hushed voice was behind me—Parminder's. I'd never heard Parminder lower her voice before and, listening to her, I had a strange feeling, the first stirring of what was to frighten me so much in the hours to come.

"We're hardly getting any further down," she hissed.

"He's doing his best," Tanni answered.

"But that's not good enough, is it? And it's getting more dangerous for him. He's weakening. Do you think the beauty will still work after Thomas is dead? I mean, if he was to die—an accident, or the heat, or whatever— perhaps his beauty would continue to function. Maybe we could still drag his dead body down with us."

Tanni did not reply.

"His bones would melt eventually, I suppose," Parminder said.

I swallowed hard. My instinctive reaction was to jump up at once and confront her. The so-casual way she'd mentioned my possible death outraged me. But—should it have? What was my purpose, after all? Maybe Parminder was right. Maybe it was simply to go down with the Unearthers until I ran out of strength and died.

Would my beauty survive my death? I doubted it, but I couldn't be certain. I thought about Milo, about his duty in the clouds, to wait for the Roar and fight it. Perhaps my responsibility was to descend with the Unearthers as far as I could, and then let them cart my dead body down even further, hoping to eke some final slivers of beauty out of it.

Perhaps—but I wasn't quite ready to accept that yet. I lifted my head, and found Parminder staring at me. Her eyes were hooded beneath the glistening bronze brows. As I looked at her, I'm not sure why, but for the first time since joining the Unearthers I realized that I was alone down here. There's no Walter, I thought. Here under the earth, I only had Tanni.

"It's okay, Thomas," he said. "Ignore Parminder. There'll be no more ridiculous talk of hauling dead bodies anywhere. Besides, if you're dead, your beauty dies with you. That's right, isn't it?"

There was something about the way he turned as he said it that made me answer the way I did. I don't know what it was, a flicker behind his eyes.

"Yes," I said. I said it as loudly and clearly as I could. "Yes, it does. If I die, it goes with me. All my beauty dies as well. Absolutely. All of it."

I didn't dare meet his eye for the next few seconds. What was happening? Surely I'd misunderstood the expression on Tanni's face. I must have. After all, hadn't he taken care of me down here? Hadn't he made certain I was fed and watered and properly looked after?

He chatted briefly in private with Parminder, and afterwards came over to sit beside me the way he'd always done in the past.

"I know you're doing your best for us," he said. "Don't take any notice of Parminder."

A flash of anger crossed Parminder's face. Then she did something that frightened me more than anything I'd seen from her before.

She made herself smile at me.

You could see it, the effort she put into that smile. A tight, sweet smile. There was something completely false about it. A muscle in her cheek twitched and twitched. On the left side of her head a tuft of hair was missing. It must have been yanked out during one of her drilling shifts, but I don't think she'd even noticed.

I got up and walked around the cave, suddenly half out of my mind.

What was going on? I didn't even want to think about it; the possibilities scared me too much.

I needed to be by myself, to think, so I started wandering around the cave, pretending to stretch my legs. That's when I worked out what had been bothering me for so long about Second Camp: there wasn't any food. I hadn't seen any in the drill-face tunnel or linked passages, either. That meant the Unearthers had been drilling without eating for at least a day.

I faced Parminder. The fixed smile was still there. Something was definitely wrong with her.

"Aren't you hungry?" I said. "Even yesterday you didn't eat much, and you've been working flat out. You must be starving by now."

"The work's more important than food," Parminder said. And then she did this: she glanced at Tanni, as if seeking his advice, as if asking, *Was that the correct thing to say to him?*

With all the hair rising on my neck, I turned towards Tanni; and when I did I wished I hadn't. Because although he tried to hide it, I saw a look that wasn't one I recognized. A guarded look. Oh, Tanni, I'd have given anything not to have seen that from you then.

"If you're worried about yourself, Thomas," Parminder said, "we have food for you here."

"I'm not worried about that," I told her, still staring at Tanni. "I'm thinking about the Unearthers. Maybe the older ones can go without food for this long, but what about the younger kids?"

"They don't need food for now," Tanni said. "They'll get by."

That stopped me cold. The Tanni I knew would never have said it.

I turned away from him, and saw a drill-team enter Second Camp from below. One of them, a teenage girl, bent down to wipe some dust off her foot, and by the light shining off her face I saw something. It had been partially hidden under an old shirt. A boy. I hadn't seen him earlier because he no longer glowed. He couldn't have been much older than five, and from the twisted way he was lying there on his face I knew at once that he was dead. Under him, as if hurriedly tucked there, was a girl, also dead. His drill-partner, I realized. Joined with him at the hand.

The fact that these two deaths had gone unmentioned was awful enough, but the truly gruesome aspect was the way the rest of the Unearthers in the cave reacted to the bodies. Several teams were sitting down near the dead boy and girl. They saw the bodies there, and weren't bothered by them at all. They didn't care enough even to move away or cover the dead faces properly.

Tanni spotted what I'd seen. "It happens," he said quickly. "A blowout. Occasionally we hit a pocket of explosive gas. We're drilling so fast we haven't got time to be careful. It's dreadful, but—"

"But considering the conditions, acceptable," Parminder said. "We've only lost these two and one more pair. The second pair are alive, but might as well be dead, because they can't drill anymore."

I stared at her, then at Tanni, dread seeping through me.

"What's . . . changed?" I murmured. I moved away from them; I couldn't help myself. "Since you left me on the surface . . . came down here . . . what's happened to each of you?"

Neither Tanni nor Parminder replied, and in the silence that followed another girl and her drill-partner entered the cave. They expelled dust at high speed through their nostril slits, then I watched them simply walk over the dead bodies. They did it as if the boy and girl were nothing more than mounds of earth. None of the other Unearthers cared. I glanced at Parminder, and got her smile again.

"You were supposed to clear them out of the way!" she

growled at two boys. "He wasn't meant to—"

Tanni jabbed her ribs, and she broke off.

"See them?" I said. "Is that right, Parminder? Is that what you were going to say, before Tanni slapped you back? No, I wasn't meant to, was I."

I could see Tanni trying to recover the situation, think of the right remark to placate me, but how could he? Too late for that. But I almost wanted him to, because my whole world was falling to pieces. I wanted to appeal to him. I still wanted to trust him.

"This is wrong," I said. "Something's . . . controlling you."

"The creature below," he said. "Listen, Thomas: it's a good thing, it really is."

"Oh, I see. A good thing, is it? Two of you die, and no one cares. A couple more can't drill, so forget about them, they're useless! And it doesn't matter if no one's eating. As long as you can still dig, of course—dig down to whatever's manipulating you. The *good* thing."

A fleeting bewilderment, something less than metal, slid for a second across Tanni's face. Then it was gone, and when he returned his gaze to me his expression was identical to Parminder's.

"Don't question us," she said tersely. "Your task is to give your beauty to those chosen to be the second defenders. That's what we are."

"Oh, Tanni," I said, appealing directly to him, "Tanni . . . you're not. How can you be the second defenders? That dead boy and girl over there . . . you're becoming something else, something terrible. But you can't even see it, can you? Listen to me—"

"We need you with us," he pleaded, but his face didn't match his voice.

I backed further away from him. "None of you reacted to the Roar when I was at the drill-head. I knew that was wrong! None of you even mentioned it. What do you think it means, Tanni, when you're no longer scared by the sound of the Roar?"

"We need you," he repeated, even less convincingly.

I shook my head. "No. It's not me you need. I know what it is. You've told me often enough. It's my beauty, isn't it? That's what you're after. And you're getting it, too, aren't you! You're getting all you want from helpful little Thomas. You've been playing me along, haven't you, Tanni?"

I thought back over everything that had happened between me and the Unearthers. Had they always been using me? No. Not at the beginning. Parminder had been horrified by the early changes, and Tanni had barely held the Unearthers together. Their bodies had been changing, but their minds on that first day had still been their own.

What I did next, I'd promised myself I would never do to these children.

I held part of my beauty back.

The reaction from the Unearthers was instantaneous.

"No!" Parminder raged. "You can't! Don't you dare do

that!" She raised her free arm. Only Tanni prevented her from striking my face. She spat at me instead.

"You idiot!" Tanni shouted at her. "You idiot! I told you to let me do the talking! I told you!" He cut her arm. As if her skin was nothing more than another piece of irritating rock, he sliced her. She screamed, but took it. All the Unearthers in the cave were staring at me now. Not one of them was bothered by what Tanni had done to Parminder.

She wanted nothing more than to hit out at me. You could see it. Parminder stared me up and down, furious and exasperated, a bronze hate-filled face. Her unbreakable head was sheened with sweat. Her huge hands were like battering rams.

I turned back to Tanni. "That stuff back up there on the surface, all the jokiness with Parminder when you came out of your hole. It was all just a pretense, wasn't it? To make sure I came down here. You didn't want to take any chances on that, did you?"

Tanni studied me coolly. All the counterfeit friendliness was gone now. He assessed me, obviously wondering how to obtain my cooperation.

"No," I said. "You're not getting any more. No more beauty. None. Do you hear me?"

"Give us it! Give us *all* of it!" Parminder yelled at me, all fakery dropped at last.

"You're on your own down here," Tanni said calmly. "Don't resist us, Thomas. You haven't got any choice."

Was that true? I looked for a way to withhold my beauty. It wouldn't be easy. My beauty wasn't designed to be withheld; it was meant to flow freely out from me. I tried, anyway. I clenched my teeth and put all my concentration into preventing the beauty from entering the Unearthers. And it worked. For a few seconds I made it work, but even those few seconds were hard, because my own beauty resisted me. A cold mouth from the Unearthers was sucking at it. I could only keep it inside with extreme difficulty.

"Good," Parminder said to Tanni. "He's obviously not going to be able to stop us from getting it, or not much of it. We'll leave him here. Nothing important's changed. His beauty will continue doing its job, as long as we keep him alive."

Tanni shook his head, and for a moment, a pathetic moment, I actually thought he was going to take pity on me. Then I saw the new lid slide across one of his eyes, and his face was only metal, and I realized that if there was any spark of the old Tanni left it was buried deep inside that steel.

"Take me back to the surface," I demanded.

Ignoring me, Tanni addressed the rest of the Unearthers. "Keep digging exactly as we've been doing. But I want the lead teams at the drill seam alternating in shorter shifts every fifteen minutes."

"Is *he* coming down with us?" one boy said. "We need him."

"Yes," Tanni said, patting me the way someone might pat a favored dog. "Thomas will be coming, all right." He raised his free hand, and I instinctively put up my arms to protect myself—but Tanni was only motioning to one of the drill-teams. "Now if I really wanted to hurt you, Thomas," he said, "just lifting up your arms and cringing like that isn't going to stop me, is it?"

NINE

that larger darkness

HELEN

The morning after Walter's birthday celebration Emily and Freda slept peacefully on their mattress—some respite for them, at last, from those crazed dreams of the sea.

I dressed quietly and went outside. It was an overcast day, with diesel fumes drifting in from ships docking all along the coast. Whole nations of children were still trying to make it here. Coldharbour itself could no longer contain them all, so they spilled inland, taking up space wherever it was available in the nearer towns and countryside. And the Barrier traveled outward with them. All the time it pushed the parents further back.

Recently two Polish girls, sisters, had arrived in our area. They sat near me, their faces lined with exhaustion, looking up in relief every minute or so at Milo, not quite able to believe they'd made it. With no commercial ships available, they'd set off from Skórzyno near the Baltic Sea in only a home-constructed raft. Against a sea-storm lasting six hours the sisters had held together a sail made from bedroom sheets, a fence stake, and nails.

Millions of stories like this. Millions of them.

I glanced across at Walter, who was helping some teenagers secure the pegs of tents. The adults still couldn't find a way inside the Barrier, but at last they were sending in supplies of materials with which to make basic shelters.

Walter built most of those in our area. His now much-reduced selection of visitors clustered around his legs as he worked, feeling special. Jenny was one of many eyeing them jealously. She hadn't spoken to Walter or even acknowledged his existence all morning.

I checked into her mind and was shocked to find this: Thomas, sitting against a wall, his fists clenched, holding off a boy with a face of steel.

As I strode over to her she sniffed, picking at her dressing gown. "I'm messy," she protested. "Look!" She showed me the mud stains on her clothes and ankles. "It's not fair! I can't get it off! I need a bath. I'm dirty, like a boy! I can't get clean!"

"I know," I said. "It doesn't matter. Nobody minds. It's just mud." I desperately wanted to question her about Thomas, but noticing the state of her gown had distracted her. I stroked her hair, wishing suddenly that I had a comb for it, because that's what Jenny wanted more than anything. When she'd settled down a little, I tried again.

"Is Thomas in danger, Jenny? Is that what you're seeing?"

She picked at her fingernails, giving me a shy smile.

"I like Thomas," she said.

"What do you like about him?"

"I like his beauty."

"Do you?"

"Yes. I want it."

She looked bashfully away, then back. There it was again in her mind: the steel face of the boy I'd seen before. And this time I had a name. It briefly flashed across Jenny's thoughts. Not a child's name: Unearther.

"Who *is* that boy?" I whispered. "Do you know him?"

"There are bad people," Jenny said.

"In what way bad?"

"They do bad things."

"How do we stop them?"

"I don't know." She fiddled awkwardly with her hands.

"Jenny, this is important. Do you know where Thomas is?"

"No."

She abruptly jumped up and ran off, all thoughts of Thomas instantly gone again. I sighed, following her. She'd gone off to play with her new play toy. Fashioned out of mud again, it was a seabird of some kind. I could hardly blame her for wanting it—she missed her home toys—but I felt like confiscating it. I felt like shaking her until she told me what I needed to know.

What *was* Jenny? What kind of gift did she have? She seemed to have predicted what would happen to the twins. If that was true, could this appalling-faced Unearther boy in her mind be real? Was Thomas actually with him now, being threatened?

I stayed outside for a few minutes longer, questioning Jenny without getting any more answers. All I sensed from her was that Thomas was in terrible danger. Finally I returned to the shack, intending to ask the twins to use their speed to go on a search around Coldharbour. If anyone could pick up clues that might lead us to Thomas, it was them.

But Emily and Freda had another journey in mind.

They met me at the door, already dressed, looking pale and drained. I realized at once that both girls had come to a decision.

"Don't be stupid!" I snapped. "You're still recovering! You can't go back to the sea. Look at you both! You're nowhere near ready!"

"We 'ave to be," Freda murmured.

"You can't even walk properly," I said, staring at Emily.

"I won't need to where we're going," she answered, her fingers tenderly brushing Freda's arm.

I wanted to stop them. I knew their minds were made up, but they were still so weak, their arms poking even thinner than before through their dress sleeves. "Walter won't let you," I said, using the first argument that came into my head. "He'll be dead set against it. He'll never agree to take you back to the shore. And there's no way you can walk all the way on your own, Emily. Even with Freda's help, you won't make it."

Emily put a finger to my lips.

"Shush," she said gently. "Shush, now. We know you care. It's all right. Walts won't want to let uz go, but ee'll accept it if you will."

"Trust uz," Freda said.

I stood there, frantically trying to think of better arguments.

"We 'ave to reach it," Emily said. "We can't wait anymore. Of all people, you know that. Can't you tell there's no more time? We 'ave to free the Protector. Before the Roar gets 'ere, we 'ave to. Or try, anyways." She straightened her back and looked me directly in the eye. "We're scared all right," she admitted. "Course we are. We won't pretend anything else. But so what? Who ain't? We're not the only ones shivering, are we?" She put her hand to my cheek. "You're the same, Helen. You're scared too, ain't you? If anything you're scared worse than uz."

"What do you mean?" I asked.

But I understood exactly what Emily meant, and I lowered my eyes.

"You can't help being frightened of it," Freda whispered. "But go there anyway. Go out to the Roar. See what it is. Only you can do that."

"She will," Emily said. "In her own time. She don't need uz to tell her." And then, gathering herself, she offered me a strained smile. "Walts is out there," she sighed, peering through a crack in the door. "Ee won't take it well. It's best if we both go to 'im, Freda. Will you come too, Helen? Ee'll only be straight over to you otherwise."

The three of us left the shack. As soon as Walter saw our expressions, he somehow knew. Putting a girl hanging off his shoulder down, he advanced towards us. "No! N-no!" he said, thumping the ground. "No! No! No . . ."

"Walts!" The twins scuttled across, trying to make him understand. I joined them, but I couldn't do it with any real conviction. When Walter refused to listen I left the girls with him, returned to the shack and lay down shakily. Next thing, Dad was beside me.

"I've heard the news," he said. "Walter's refusing to take either of the girls, unless you tell him he has to do it."

"I've already told him, Dad."

"He wasn't convinced, then. He needs you to tell him again."

I started to get up, but Dad held my arm.

"You don't think the twins are going to survive this time, do you?"

I didn't reply.

He knelt down beside me. "Listen: just because you can follow what's in all our heads, that doesn't make you responsible for every decision made. Whatever happens, it's the twins' decision. They've made up their own minds.

If anything goes wrong, it's not your fault, Helen."

I stayed silent.

"Besides," he said, "there's nothing you can do to stop them. Their minds are definitely made up."

But Dad was wrong about that. Despite their words, the twins trusted my judgment. If I advised them strongly enough not to go, or to at least delay going, I knew I could make them listen. Should I do that? Why? So that I felt better? For how long would it make me feel better? Until I next heard the Roar?

"I've offered the twins some food," Dad said. "Something to sustain them on the journey. They won't take it, though. I'm not sure why."

"They'll be sick if they eat now," I said. "That's what they're worried about—choking under the waves."

I confronted Walter. I stood in front of him and looked into those huge disbelieving eyes of his and I told him again to let the twins leave. And as I did so, I felt something completely new from Walter. It made me suddenly want to cry, because he hated me in that moment. For those few seconds he hated me. Not because there was any malice in him, but because he could sense I wasn't convinced myself. He knew I wasn't sure, and he couldn't understand why I was making him do this.

Overhead the skies had cleared, and a crisp wind whistled under Milo's wings. Jenny—unwillingly, still not talking to Walter at all—climbed aboard him. Dad stood alongside, ready to set off, while the rest of us waited for Walter to bend down to allow us onto his back. He nearly didn't. Then, still furious with me, he picked us up, faced into the breeze and set off towards the sea. I'd seen Walter move over the ground with purpose before. I'd even seen him travel with the same grim expression he did now. But on that occasion it had been to save Milo's life, not endanger two others. His feet moved sluggishly across Coldharbour—a deliberately ponderous tread that would give us time to change our minds.

No one spoke on the journey. I looked at Dad. From her perch on Walter's neck, Jenny clutched her bird doll and gazed up at her brother. The twins stared fixedly ahead at the approaching sea. As for Walter, he moved as reluctantly towards the waves as if death itself was waiting for us.

We reached the beach at last, and this time there was no beginner's fear from the twins, no dallying in the shallows. They slipped immediately down Walter's legs to the deeper water. For a moment their heads and shoulders bobbed on the surface. Then, as they prepared to submerge, Walter couldn't help himself—he reached for them.

"Walts, it's all right," Emily said, rubbing her cheeks against his hands. "Whatever's the matter? It's all right. It is. It's what we want."

"You nearly d-died before!" he blurted. "You know you did!"

"Ah, what are yer doing, beautiful boy?" Freda said, when Walter wouldn't let go. "Don't yer know we're going where we 'ave to be?"

Both girls threw their arms around him, then lowered themselves down into the water.

Seeing that there was no chance of persuading the twins, Walter gave them one of his lopsided grins. He held that spectacular effort-filled smile on his face.

"I'll w-wait for you," he said. "Like b-before. I'll wait h-here for you."

"No, don't," Emily said. "I . . . we'll . . . be a long time, Walts."

"I d-d-don't mind. I'll—" Suddenly Walter exploded. "You don't think you're c-coming back, do you? That's why you said that!"

Only a squeal from Emily stopped him from dragging them back out of the water. "Please, Walts," she said. "We may be back. Mind Helen and Jenny. They're yours to care for now."

Walter nodded heavily, his chin falling against his chest.

Freda glanced at the silver-flecked waves, then solemnly at her sister.

"It's time, Emms."

"I know." Emily attempted a smile, but now that it was time to put her head under the water her face was white.

"Are yer ready?" Freda asked her softly.

"I am. Hold my hand."

Freda did so, then changed her mind, caught full hold of Emily's waist and drew them both under the waves.

It took ages to persuade Walter to leave the beach. We were half-forgotten on his shoulders as he lugged us home, and when we got back he went straight inside his hut. Even his visitors could tell that he needed to be alone, and for the rest of that morning they looked after each other.

I waited outside, discussing things with Dad for hours. After that I just wandered around our area on my own for a while, listening in on the thoughts of children in Cold-harbour. I was hoping for a clue to Thomas's whereabouts, but there was nothing. Where are you? I wondered. How could you be hidden so completely from me?

Finally a few stars appeared in the sky, glowing dimly against Milo's silver, and I went back inside the shack. The twins' mattress lay horribly empty next to mine. Dad came in soon afterwards. Without speaking he lay on his back, folded his hands under his head and stared up at the ceiling. I listened in on his thoughts. Take a snapshot of any parent outside the Barrier, and they were all thinking the same thing as Dad: that they couldn't protect their own children. They only had to hear a child, any child, describe the approach of the Roar, and they knew that. They knew there was absolutely nothing they could do to stop it.

"It doesn't matter," I whispered to him. "I need you as you are, Dad. Just stay that way." I leaned against him, and for a while I even managed to doze off in his arms.

I woke up thinking about the Roar. A few days before, on my way into Coldharbour for the first time, I'd accidentally made contact with its mind. That touch had been so chilling I never wanted to go back there again. But if we were to learn anything useful about our enemy, I'd have to. The twins had been right to remind me. I'd always known I'd have to return to the Roar's mind. I was just never ready.

So—somewhere else first. Somewhere safer; closer to home.

Milo.

There he was, stationed in the high clouds.

I thought about his eyes. They were open, constantly alert. People saw the eye facing down towards Coldharbour, but no one saw the upturned eye. It was forever fixed on the stars. Milo left it there because he knew that was the direction the Roar would come from. The upturned eye never blinked. Milo didn't allow it to; he didn't dare.

As for his mind, it teemed with defensive strategies. Over and over again he rehearsed varied tactical positions and battle postures he could use against the Roar. And over and over he rehearsed the use of his wings as well—a thousand ways he might deploy them to defend us. Sometimes, in his mind, Milo practiced confronting the onslaught of the Roar directly, full on in the blackness of space. On other occasions he stayed in our skies, hardening his frame like armor. Once I'd caught him considering how to fight on even if the Roar destroyed his wings and most of his body.

Milo shook with the effort to understand all the possible ways the Roar might attack us in time.

I couldn't follow what the defensive strategies in his mind meant. To me, they were more like equations than words, more like shifting mathematical models. And suddenly I realized something: I was *never meant* to understand. Because if I did, so might the Roar. The first time I'd looked into its hungry mind it had looked back like a horror into mine. It had found a way to get inside my thoughts.

If I understood Milo's defenses, the Roar could steal the information.

I pondered that awhile, then roused myself. I wasn't ready to go to the Roar yet, but I needed to test myself further. Come on, I thought. Somewhere less comfortable. Where are they?

I searched for the twins. I'd never attempted a probe underwater before, and felt sure I wouldn't find them, but I did: two girls, holding hands in the dark sea. I drew away at once, the pain of being inside both girls' minds at the same time too much to bear.

I made myself go back to Freda. There she was, still holding onto Emily's waist, not daring to let go. She was so cold. The sea swayed like ice under her fingernails and, beside her, Emily was weakening. Down Freda went, always down, shaking with concern for Emily, holding her and pressing on, her legs kicking ever more frantically into the abyss. For over an hour I stayed with her, until she was so deep I could barely detect her.

That's when I felt Freda's tears shed in the ocean.

For she had found it. A manacled creature. A vast thing that shook in its bindings; that trembled for them in wait; that flexed and flexed. For a moment I felt the twins dive longingly towards it, their fingers running like a welcome across the miles and miles of its body, their hearts jumping when they felt it heave.

Then the twins went ever deeper, and I couldn't follow them anymore. I lay there crying, with Dad feeling useless beside me.

"Hold me," I told him.

"What are you doing?" he rasped.

"Just hold me."

There was only one place left to go now. The first time I'd felt the mind of the Roar, I'd recoiled in terror. I knew I probably would again, but there was no choice. Gripping Dad's arm, I gathered myself and reached out. I passed through the anxious minds of Coldharbour. I passed beyond the bordering ocean, beyond emptying countries, beyond anything on this world. Space: I went out there. On a hunt for a killer I strayed into that larger darkness.

And there she was.

I realized one thing at once: she knew me. The Roar knew I was there; she recognized me. I wasn't a stranger. From my first visit to her mind, she remembered. A shaft of fear ripped through me then, and if the creature we called the Roar could have smiled as we do, I think in that moment she might have.

There were two others with her, two smaller part-formed creatures, the ones she called her newborn.

What exactly were they? I felt in their minds, and found them hibernating. It was the only way for them to survive the cold of space and the agonies of starvation. For a moment I felt what it was like to be one of them, a stomach shrunk with emptiness and pain, and a terrible pity drew me to linger among the newborn.

And then one of them made a mistake. It opened its mouth at me, and I realized that I'd been tricked. I'd been tricked into staying with them long enough for the Roar to sift at my thoughts for information about Milo and any other defenses we might have. I broke contact at once, and the Roar screamed in fury. She and her newborn reached out with a scream that flailed every child in the world.

TEN

i am not alone

THE ROAR

The Roar permitted Helen to flee.

"Follow her," demanded one of her newborn. "Kill her."

"No," the Roar answered. "She discovered nothing from us, while we found out all we need. She may still be useful. You must learn when to kill at once and when to delay a kill."

The newborn whose mistake had revealed them stayed silent. Normally the Roar would have automatically fed it to the other newborns after such a blunder, but, since only two remained, its punishment would have to be more subtle.

While she devised that punishment the Roar moved in an undeviating path towards the Earth. It was close now, but she remained cautious, camouflaging her skin to match the dark of space, and always looking out for the telltale glowing trails of the Protectors. Where were they?

It had been so long since she last saw one of their fast-moving bodies.

In her youth she had hunted down many Protectors. The remembered satisfaction of that: to have trusted killers at your side, and come upon a lone Protector, and watch it fly in panic, and over countless years chase it down and butcher it. Indeed, no one had caught more than she. As the leader of an assassin-team, her sole purpose had been their killing.

The last one she had seen had been *this* world's Protector.

She recalled when she first encountered it, rising like a silver shadow from the moon to confront her. The Roar was alone at the time, though still in peak physical condition: magnificently strong, well rested and newly fed, a battle-veteran with all her poisons intact.

Even so, she had hesitated to take on a Protector by herself.

To commence the battle the Protector had lifted up from the moon and extended its silver body like a shield across the Earth.

"I am not alone."

That was the first thing it said to her, and a mistake. She put out her detections and knew the Protector was lying. That meant it was afraid. It had also waited in plain view on the moon, instead of hiding on the sunless side and launching an attack against her vulnerable rear-flukes. That meant it was inexperienced.

Knowing that, she roared once to steady herself—and attacked.

She and her enemy were well matched. The Roar had fought many Protectors before, but never on her own against an opponent of almost equal strength. Sometimes for centuries at a stretch they clenched one another fiercely. Other times they rested, and during those times she would whisper to the Protector, trying to weaken its resolve. It was young, this Protector; perhaps it could be convinced to flee if she injured it enough. No. It did not flee. And so, for ages more, she and the Protector fought: strength against strength, skill on skill, patience and fury.

It was Carnac, her offspring, who made the decisive difference.

During all the battle with the Protector the Roar had carried him inside her—the first of her newborn, and the best. And what a healthy thick offspring he had been when he burst out of her body at last! The Protector had known its fate. It had watched Carnac growing inside her with mounting alarm, knowing that once he was born it would no longer stand a chance.

How desperately the Protector had fought her in those last years!

The Roar would never have defeated the Protector without Carnac. It was he who finally helped her subdue it. The moment he tore himself loose from her belly the Roar sent him at the Protector's single great eye—blinding it.

Nevertheless, the Protector had continued to guard the world below. Ignoring its injuries, guessing at where she was, it desperately placed its body between the Roar and the planet. Finally, she and Carnac bit off enough parts of it to drag the Protector's colossal bulk down to the surface of the Earth. There she attempted to kill it, but it was difficult—she was exhausted, and a Protector will not quickly die when it has a world to defend.

Too weak to kill the Protector outright, the Roar had to decide what to do. She didn't dare leave it on the surface. Any passing Protector was bound to see it. So she dragged her enemy into the deepest ocean of the world and tried to drown it. When the Protector would not drown, she held it down while Carnac chewed it into submission enough to clamp and bind it until the Protector could no longer move.

There she left it, intending to return to the Roar home world, feed, recover her strength, and finish the Protector off at a later time.

But before that she had to hide Carnac. He was not yet swift enough to evade the other Protectors in open space. First he must grow. To do that he must eat. To eat he must wait. This world was still a new one. There was primitive plant life, but not enough for a meal. Carnac needed to wait until the animals grew and spread across the world.

Given time, there would be ample to fill his appetite.

Until then, she must conceal him from the Protectors. So, with her teeth, the Roar bit through to the white-hot core of the world, and there she placed her firstborn. The heat cracked Carnac's skin, and he screamed. He understood what she was doing, but even so it was not possible for Carnac to go easily into those fires. At the last moment, as she sealed the rock above him, even knowing it was for his own good, he twisted to get at her, to escape.

"Soon you will be strong enough to free yourself," she told him. "And when you are there will be abundant food on this world waiting for you."

With him shrieking at her from the furnace of the Earth, she departed.

It was a long return journey to the Roar home world, and when she arrived there was a shock awaiting her: the Protectors surrounded it. All she could see were their silver bodies. So she wrapped herself around a dead planet and hid, waiting for them to leave. Time passed and she slowed down her heart. She slept. When she woke again the Protectors were still encircling the home world.

Yet the Roar had to eat, and finally there was nowhere else to go—she headed back to the planet where she had left Carnac. Only starvation led her to return. There was only the slightest chance that after Carnac had emerged from the core he would have left enough food to sustain her.

But then, nearing the Earth, she had sensed him—still there! Still in the core! But how? He should have broken free ages before and taken his pick of the food. There could be only one explanation.

The Protector was still alive—and stronger than she ever imagined.

After all this time the Roar had almost forgotten about the Protector, believing it long ago shriveled and dead. But it had held on to life, just as she had done. From its sunken imprisonment, from the depths, despite its weakness, the Protector still commanded enough will to hold Carnac in.

It also meant that the animals would have multiplied on this world beyond anything seen before. What a wealth of eating would be there! For many years the Roar had anticipated that meal.

The children intrigued her. A planet had never been left for so long that creatures like them had developed. Complex creatures. Intelligent and adaptable. However, their bodies were small and fragile, no match for a Roar.

The Protector, naturally, had done what it could to help them. Knowing she was coming, it had chosen one of them and lifted him into the sky as a silver child. Even now it was in his mind, teaching him all it knew about how to defend the world. The Protector had also made the boy glow to attract the other children, bringing them to a single location where they could best be shielded. In a feeble attempt at rescue, the Protector had even enticed children under the ocean.

Two females were with it now, cleaning the marine debris off its eye.

But her firstborn, Carnac, had not been idle either.

Though the Protector's will held him back, the Roar realized that Carnac, too, had some influence over the children. He had dominated a few. He had also discovered a male child with an unusual gift, and used that child to give the others drills, and strengthen their bodies so that they might cut a path down to him, and free him. Thomas. That one resistant child was now the only force stopping the others from reaching him.

The Roar called out to Carnac and, hearing her for the first time in so long, he returned her call passionately. The Protector also heard them both, and the Roar had this gratification: sensing it shake with fear in its water-wasted flesh.

And later that day came the best news of all. Her newborn understood first. Both of them began running frantically over her body, nipping her flesh in their excitement.

"We can see it!" they cried. "We can see it! The world!"

The Roar hesitated to believe them, but her stomachs, from some distant memory, recalled their purpose and reignited. Feeling the fires start up, the Roar let the blood sluice into all the neglected regions of her body. She reanimated her olfactory glands. She pumped liquid into her jaw. She reinflated her poison sacs. She raised her eyes from their torpor, and at last was able to see again. Giving due care to each organ and limb, she permitted every part of her immense body a slow and careful awakening. After the prolonged period of disuse, one of her clench-limbs refused to open out, but the others gripped each other, reminding themselves of their purpose.

And then she roared. She opened up the hinges of her skull and roared with an abandon she had only dared in her days of glory.

All at once her appetite was fresh. Food. She needed it. She wanted nothing more than to lick everything from the approaching world. She was not close enough yet for that, but she could make a start. Widening her jaw, the Roar gathered up her lungs and prepared her throat to receive the first of the children.

ELEVEN

the shield

HELEN

It was nighttime in Coldharbour when Milo's warning came.

Within seconds, Dad and I were half-dressed and out of the shack. The same thing was happening across Coldharbour, a rising tide of fear as all the children looked up to Milo, trying to understand.

His words were deafening, like an angel with a message of terror.

"GET INSIDE!" his voice boomed from the sky. "THOSE WITH ACCESS TO SHELTER, USE IT. ALL OTHERS TIE YOURSELVES DOWN. OLDER CHILDREN PROTECT YOUNGER ONES. SECURE THE YOUNGEST FIRST."

Over and over he called out to us, in multiple languages.

"GIVE THE SMALLEST CHILDREN PRIORITY. PROTECT THE LIGHTEST INFANTS. PLACE

THEM IN SOLID STRUCTURES OR ATTACH THEM TO HEAVY OBJECTS. TIE YOURSELVES DOWN. . . ."

Teenagers rubbing sleep out of their eyes scrambled to get younger children inside makeshift huts, shacks, and tents. Others searched for rope, straps, belts, wire, or anything else they could find to fasten down the smallest kids. They had no idea why Milo was asking them to do it, but they trusted him.

Dad motioned for three youngsters to come to him. "Why the lightest?" he asked me, tying them down. "Helen, what's going on? There aren't anywhere near enough ropes for all these children!"

"It's the Roar," I said.

His eyes widened. "Get into our shack!" he shouted across at a little girl, then turned to me. "How long have we got?"

"It's *here*, Dad."

Walter was besieged. Dozens of terrified youngsters were screaming for his attention. He gathered Jenny and as many others as he could in his arms, and delivered them to his hut or to older children with more rigid tents or shacks. But it was impossible for Walter to help all those reaching out their arms for him; there was always another one, a little further away. He stopped for a moment, stood up, and bellowed at the top of his voice: "F-find a partner! Find someone to help you! Find the nearest p-person and ask them to tie you down. Find s-someone to help! Older children, r-raise your hands, so you can be seen!"

His voice was almost drowned out by the swell of panic spreading across Coldharbour. At the drop-off points, mothers and fathers were clawing at the Barrier, trying to get inside to help their own children. From all parts of Coldharbour a huge tide of youngsters was heading in the opposite direction—towards their parents.

That was a mistake. Milo saw what was happening and issued a new message:

"DO NOT RUN! STAY WHERE YOU ARE! FIND SOMEONE YOUNGER TO PROTECT. THE SMALLEST CHILDREN WILL BE THE FIRST TARGETS. I WILL FORM A DEFENSE BUT IT WILL TAKE TIME. DO NOT RUN. . . ."

The child-families took up the challenge. Throughout Coldharbour they were on the lookout, soaking up as many stray youngsters as they could. With no adults to guide them, the leaders made decisions themselves, just as they had done on the long journey into Coldharbour.

Milo's message thundered down relentlessly. It did not stop for several minutes. Then he paused, and when Milo began again he said this:

"THERE IS NO MORE TIME. ALL HEAVIER-BODIED PEOPLE OFFER YOUR STRENGTH TO OTHERS. HOLD DOWN THOSE SMALLEST CHILDREN STILL NOT SECURED. PREPARE YOURSELVES. . . ."

Dad was some distance from me, pushing two more boys into our already crowded shack.

"Helen, what are you doing?" he shouted across. "Get inside our place!"

"There's no room left."

"Then *make* some room. You're not staying out here!"

"What about you?"

"I'll follow you in. Go on!"

"THERE IS NO MORE TIME. HOLD DOWN THE YOUNGEST. IT IS BEGINNING. . . ."

Dad planted his knees and elbows firmly in the soil and motioned to a girl, who scrambled under his belly. All across Coldharbour bigger children offered themselves up in the same way.

"Get inside, Helen!" Dad screamed over his shoulder. "Will you do what I tell you!"

"I'm not throwing someone else out of the shack!"

"Then . . . come *here*."

I started towards him, but stopped when Milo moved. It was a fractional movement, a twist of his torso.

"What is it?" Dad yelled.

"Milo's preparing to shield us," I said.

"Shield us from what?"

But Dad could guess, and when everyone saw what Milo did next they all knew. It was his eye. Milo's left eye had always gazed down on us. It was forever trained on the children of Coldharbour. Now Milo swept it up until both eyes were tilted away from us, towards the sky. His face was set. The wind moved over his wings, and a groan of terror spread across Coldharbour.

"It's coming!" someone shrieked.

In the hysteria that followed I couldn't get close to Dad; too many people were running in front of us.

"*Walter!*" Dad cried. Moments later a giant hand closed around my neck. "G-got you," Walter said, leaping towards his hut, but I shouted, "No time! On the ground!"

He dropped on all fours, sweeping me under him along with several other children.

Then each of us heard a sound like the tearing apart of all things.

"The Roar!" someone wailed.

But it was not. I gazed up. Milo was furiously dragging his wings across the sky.

"What's he doing?" Dad called out to me. "Is he hurt?"

"No, it's not that."

Milo was pumping blood into his wings. He drew them backward and forward, like a storm of wind lashing the sky. Faster and faster he beat them, until they started to grow: twice their previous size, then three times that, more. But Milo knew they needed to be much larger to protect us all.

The first object to be removed by the Roar was taken moments later.

It was just a scrap of paper, and I'd barely have spotted it except for the way the paper moved. It didn't flap about idly. It rose directly up into the sky. More items followed, hundreds of the smallest, lightest things—cardboard, wrappers, food, plastic bags. Within seconds anything not tied down or inside a hut, shack, or tent was ascending in a straight line from the ground. None of the inanimate objects rose for long. They were plucked up, one after another, and then discarded.

The sight was so bizarre that initially it was hard to be frightened. The sorting took place slowly. You had time, if you wanted, to walk across and catch the objects. I saw a pebble rise up from the ground. A stick followed, then dropped again. As if, I thought, the Roar is testing them—deciding if they're food.

A flower flicked up straight, like a person might stand, and shot away. A blade of grass chased after it, torn from its little root.

Suddenly everyone's hair rose on their scalps.

Then the first animal was taken.

It was someone's dog, a puppy. It yelped, forelimbs and paws scrambling for the ground. A girl quickly snatched it down before it rose too high, and suddenly everyone whose pets had followed them into Coldharbour was checking they were safe. But not all the animals in Coldharbour were pets. In flurries, as if a breeze was taking them, insects were plucked up. Voles. Mice. A nest of thick-tailed rats.

Then the seabirds began to struggle.

The black-backed gulls predominating over Coldharbour's shore were used to fending off tough changeable winds from the sea, but the force sucking at them now was no wind. A huge flock of them tried to hold themselves steady over the water. I'd never seen birds battling the way those gulls did. For over a minute they bent their wings against the force dragging them upward, and then, in a last effort, the whole shrieking flock drew together for protection. It was not enough. The Roar took them. In a single sickly motion all of the birds were sucked up into the sky. Their bodies struck one of Milo's legs, then the gulls rose ever higher until they disappeared above him. Further along the coast cormorants dived into the water, but that did not save them either. They were pulled from it. Fish too close to the surface joined them, an entire shoal lifted skyward.

A tabby cat near us was plucked up. The Roar was becoming more skilled at selecting its victims, and there was not enough time to catch it. Perhaps if Walter had lifted his arm, he might have. But it would have meant exposing the children under his body, and how could he do that?

The mewling cat floated up and away. I watched it rise five hundred feet, then a hundred more, until it clattered against the underside of Milo's body, slipping across him to the sky beyond.

Milo's wings continued to grow. You could hear the urgent blood being forced into them now, bulking them out, making them taut. But it still wasn't happening fast enough. Milo knew that no matter how well the shacks and tents were pinned to the ground or how well the youngsters were tied down, those preparations wouldn't hold off the Roar for long. His wings needed to be larger, but there was no time to make them large enough. And even if he could shield all those in and around Coldharbour, what about the rest? Billions of people were still on their way to us from all parts of the world. He could never reach out far enough for them.

Moments later we lost our first child.

I could barely see her, a little girl somewhere east of us. It was her curiosity that doomed her. She'd scrambled out from a tent, not understanding the danger, worried about what was happening to Milo. I couldn't bear to watch as she drifted up and away. Immediately, across Coldharbour, the same thing happened to dozens more of the lightest children. The mouth of the Roar, I realized, finding what it wanted. Gathering us up.

Inhaling us.

Everyone was now fighting to stay on the ground. My arm rose, and when I glanced around arms were rising everywhere, as if all of us were putting our hands up to ask a question. The hair tugged at my scalp. My foot lifted an inch or so—and I clutched Walter tightly.

"I won't l-let you go," he said.

No one else, though, had a Walter to guard them. I saw two big boys dragging his car door, trying to cover a group of youngsters caught out in the open. Across from me, Dad had instinctively lowered his body, bringing his center of gravity closer to the ground. He held steady, but his neck was being pulled up. From all parts of Coldharbour there were screams as everyone tried desperately to find something extra to cling on to.

That's when Milo made his decision.

He had waited as long as he could. He had enlarged his wings and allowed as many people as possible outside their span to scramble under them. Now he could wait no longer. He accepted the size of his wings, inadequate though they were. He drew in his legs.

And dropped from the sky.

Many people put their hands over their heads. They thought Milo, injured somehow, was going to crush us. Instead he halted, hovering no more than a building's height over our heads. Then, mantling his wings like a hawk, he made of them two great semicircular arcs and with all his strength slammed the tips into the seabed and territory surrounding Coldharbour.

The wind taking the children ended instantly—Milo's wings sealing us in. But not all the children could be saved. By the time Milo brought down his shield, some were already high in the sky. One poor boy, way up in the air over western Coldharbour, plummeted to the ground and nothing could prevent his death. Elsewhere, children fell into the sea, and people waded out to find them before they drowned. Three girls in our area had only risen a short distance and were caught by a child-family.

Above us there was no sky left. There was only the silvery underside of Milo's wings. We were shut within. Sighs of relief came from everyone as they understood the immediate danger was over, but huts and shacks lay in pieces, children, animals, and possessions strewn everywhere.

The presence of Walter ensured that we lost no one to the Roar in our area, but elsewhere dozens were missing. All around, children tethered to the ground were shakily getting to their feet. None of them, though, dared loosen their ropes yet.

A single oversized hand remained clamped on my head and wouldn't let go. "Walter," I said. "It's all right. It's over."

"Is it?"

He didn't believe me. Grudgingly loosening his grip on my face, he peered down. About a dozen trembling children were bunched up together against his chest. Jenny came bolting from his hut to join us.

Dad let go of the girl he'd been protecting, and I helped those children huddling inside our hut to find their brothers, sisters, and friends.

Afterwards, Dad came over and hugged me for several seconds without speaking. Then, once he had tested that the structure of the shack was still safe enough for us to go inside, he led me through the door. We slumped down together on the edge of a bed, slowly recovering.

"Was it the Roar?" he asked hoarsely.

"No," I said. "Not the Roar itself. Just the beginning of its appetite."

He shook his head, then saw my hands trembling and held them. "Helen, how long before it reaches us?"

"I don't know, Dad. Not long."

"Do you know what's going to happen next?"

"No."

He gazed at me. "And the twins? What about the twins?"

I knew what he was thinking. Where were they? Since I'd felt Freda running her fingers along the body of the Protector, I'd registered nothing from her or Emily.

"Can you . . . can you leave me alone for a while?" I asked.

"Why?"

"I need to be on my own, that's all."

It was obvious what I had to do next. Dad took one look at my face and recognized what it was.

"The Roar," he said huskily. "You're going back to it, aren't you?"

"There's no choice," I said. "I should have known this attack was coming! I haven't done enough to find out about it. I've got to try again, Dad. There's no one else who can. Please . . . I need you keeping other people away. It's important that no one disturbs me."

Somehow I persuaded him and he walked around our neighborhood, telling everyone to stay quiet. Then he stood guard behind the shack door, listening intently to any sounds coming from inside.

I smoothed out the creases in my blankets and sat down on my mattress. What other preparations should I make? I closed my eyes, then opened them again. I waited for my heart to calm down a little.

I didn't go to the Roar straightaway. First I went to Milo. Under his shield no one could see the tears on his face, but I knew they were there. He was in torment. Children had been lost and Milo felt responsible for that. His child-sensitive eyes saw each lost boy and girl, all the dead creamy patches of light moving through the hush of space, heading towards a throat.

I followed the children. I followed the path they took towards the Roar. I went there. I went to her.

And this time she was *not* lying in wait for me.

The Roar was still coming to terms with the surprise of Milo's shield. She hadn't realized that the influence of the Protector extended so deeply inside him. Furious, the Roar even accidentally allowed me a sight of her mortal enemy—allowed me into her thoughts to see the Protector itself. Only a glimpse, that's all I had, but even that was enough to make me understand what had made the twins' hearts stir. For I saw the Protector of old, in the early days of its conflict with the Roar, its bright body holding her back, and against it she was only a shadow.

Nevertheless, the Roar was still confident of victory. She moved on steadily towards us, ignoring the material she had sucked from the Earth. Those fragments were not enough of a meal to be worth her attention, so she gave them to one of her newborn. The other newborn got nothing.

"I am aware of you," the Roar thought.

She meant me. I knew that. I felt the minds of her newborn lock into me then, and realized that the Roar was teaching them; she was helping them to recognize my presence. But perhaps she made a mistake, because one of the newborn let slip a secret.

Her offspring. Her firstborn.

For the first time, I knew about Carnac.

There he was, cracking and blistering in the heat of the core, intent on the Unearther children he was transforming. Drill over hand he was maiming them, making them into Agatha dolls and worse, forcing them down to dig him out of the heart of the world. Only one child held them back.

Thomas.

All of Carnac's will was bent on breaking him.

And then, as I looked in the newborn's mind for more, the Roar erupted into my thoughts. I retreated, but she followed me. Her mind followed me, followed me, trying to reach into me to damage me. I had no idea she could do that, but she could.

I withdrew and she came after me.

Then she stopped. I hadn't outrun her; I simply wasn't important enough to her to chase far. Milo was her target now. She wanted to annihilate him. To do so she sent out a hammering spike, striking out at him.

And overhead, above everyone in Coldharbour, the ceiling of Milo's body buckled. Another thrust from the Roar, and great dents appeared on the undersides of his wings. For a moment Milo swayed, dizzy from the blows.

But he held the shield intact.

The Roar was not overly concerned. She had learned something about his durability, and that was useful. To get what she wanted, she realized that she only needed patience. Creeping back to the edge of her mind, I knew that from now onward her tactic would be to sap Milo's strength by attacking him steadily and relentlessly. Milo was the gateway to this world. He was our chief defense. Until the Roar reached us, she would attack him without respite.

As for the people stranded outside the shield, the Roar decided to ignore them. She could have taken their bodies if she wished—there was nothing Milo could do for them now—but she was disciplined; she focused all her energies instead on attacking the silver child. A slow, steady pounding began against Milo's outer wings. It was like the thrum of heavy rainfall, and I knew that from now onward until the Roar arrived it would never cease.

Fear gripped Coldharbour for the rest of the day. Later, with no sunset or rising stars to indicate the advent of evening, children made their own decisions about when to bed down. Milo hung like a silver brilliance over our heads, so bright at this close range that he almost burned the retinas of our eyes.

I was exhausted. I'd only slept six or seven hours in the last few days. No doubt the Roar knew that, too. I think she knew everything worth knowing about me now.

Walter remained on vigil outside our shack, alert for any danger. Once the evening drew on, he couldn't keep children away from him, of course, and he didn't try. More visitors than ever sneaked up to be near him, or at least close enough so that they could see him. Late in the night a tiny girl crawled up Walter's arm, shoving aside his hand so that she could lie next to him.

And Jenny stayed with him as well. After what had happened, I knew that Walter would never let himself be parted from her again. I didn't think Jenny would leave his embrace at all in the night, but I was wrong. During the small hours she got up, walked across to our shack, and nudged me.

"Where's Thomas?" she demanded. She carried her mud bird in one hand and her cheeks were flushed. "Where is he?"

I sat up. "Jenny . . ."

She stamped the floor in frustration. "Where is he? I want to see him! Thomas! Don't you know that? Don't you know who I mean? Don't you know? I want to see him! I want to!"

Outside, light coming from Milo shone through a

crack in the shack roof. It slanted across Jenny's face. "*Brrrrrrr*," she said. She stared ferociously at me. She showed me her teeth.

"She's not cold, is she?" Dad whispered.

"It's not that," I said.

There were two noises in Jenny's mind. One was a rumble like hail—the Roar's attack on Milo. The second noise was odd. I recognized it. I realized that it had been at the edge of my consciousness for days.

The distant sound of drills.

TWELVE

the soft words
of steel

THOMAS

How do you scare someone into submission?

Down here in the Unearther tunnels, there were lots of ways.

At first Tanni simply hauled me back to the stifling heat of the drill-head, waiting for me to crack. He obviously thought that sooner or later I wouldn't be able to stand it, and then I'd give the Unearthers all the beauty they wanted. I didn't, but it was hard to deny them, and not only because of the heat. My beauty simply wasn't ever intended to be kept back. Its natural path was always to flow out of me and into other children.

Every shred of beauty I withheld from the Unearthers cost me dearly.

The Unearthers: from the beginning I'd found that name unsettling, but at last it seemed right for them. Nothing about their modified bodies resembled children anymore. I panted away in the heat, but they all looked comfortable here. They all looked the same, too, the thickly muscled boys hardly any different from the girls. Even their personalities were becoming spookily similar. Parminder had always had a more sarcastic streak in her than Tanni, but lately, when I wasn't looking at them, I couldn't always be sure who was speaking. And they only cared about one thing: tunneling downward; digging down to reach whatever was controlling them from the depths of the Earth.

They were more machine than human now, the way the drilling never paused. No lulls or rests anymore, either. No stoppages. Whatever possessed the Unearthers drove each one onward beyond exhaustion.

My body, though, wasn't built like theirs. I had to rest, and sometimes I had no choice except to sleep as well. During those times I had no control over my beauty, and the Unearthers took what they needed from it.

I found that by taking small frequent naps I could hold it back best.

"Why don't you just go mad?" Parminder said to me, one time when I was sweating away at the drill-head. And maybe under different circumstances I would have. What stopped me was that going crazy was exactly what the Unearthers wanted. A crazy person, after all, would probably give in to pain. He'd give up his beauty merely for a promise of cooler conditions. I had no idea how to stay sane, but down inside the Unearther pits I found myself thinking about it a lot.

Helen, I thought, can you hear me? I'd been silently asking for her help since the Unearthers changed, but either the messages weren't getting through or there was no way Walter or anyone else could get safely down the drop-chutes.

The drilling never let up. Tanni and Parminder masterminded the operation, though they took frequent breaks to visit me and observe how pathetic I looked. I hated the moment of weakness I'd shown in front of Tanni earlier when I thought he was going to hit me, but I couldn't do anything about that now. I kept expecting him to threaten me again, but he didn't. He merely stood there, always uncomfortably close, waiting for me to break.

After a while I was so worn out by the effort of holding back my beauty that I couldn't survive at the sharp end of the drilling. Tanni had to keep me at or near Second Camp. I had plenty of company, though; Tanni made sure of that. He liked to bring the next shift of Unearthers up to see me before their stint at the drill-face. The shift would hang around for a while, longing for a slurp of beauty. Sometimes they got some, too—I couldn't prevent a little of it from slipping out from time to time. A close circle of Unearther bodies constantly surrounded me, eager for that to happen.

As for Tanni and Parminder, they soon stopped participating personally in the drilling. Tanni was easily the smartest of the Unearthers, and knew it was far more important to concentrate on cracking my will than grubbing around at the drill-head. He kept tempting me, as well; he'd offer rewards like a trip to the milder conditions of Base Camp or a splash of ice-cold water, if only I'd give up a bit more beauty. He even tried to *persuade* me—soft words from his metal mouth—but he'd never sounded less convincing, and I think some part of him realized that.

So he contented himself with staying nearby instead. As time went by he and Parminder rarely let me out of their sight. Food and drink were brought to me. I had to think about that. Should I take them? Maybe not. After all, if I was weak, my beauty would be weak, too, and the Unearthers would get less of it. In the end I drank the water because I couldn't bear not to, and I ate the food because I knew that without my strength I wouldn't be able to resist them at all.

Tanni never talked about Milo or the situation in Coldharbour. Anything taking place above us clearly didn't interest him. After what I'd seen already of the Unearthers, that didn't surprise me. Something else, some other power, that cold mouth below, had the Unearthers in its grip. I wished I knew what it was, but even more than that I wished that I could find a way to get the old version of Tanni back. I'd liked him so much. What was he now? Not even a boy. Another one of the Unearthers, that's all. Just another machine.

I couldn't help glancing at him occasionally, though,

hoping to see a spark of humanity return. But I waited until he wasn't looking to do so, and even then I only did it out of the corner of my eye, because I was afraid of him. The qualities I'd once so admired in Tanni—the way he handled people, his determination, his self-assurance—only made him more frightening now. He was in charge in this dark world. He gave orders as confidently as any adult I'd ever met, and while the rest of the Unearthers had occasionally questioned him before, they never did so anymore.

And how he drove them! Tanni was like a whip on their drill-hands! No more individual attention for the smaller children, no more pep talks or afternoon naps. The youngest were expected to drill their little hearts out, just like the rest. Occasionally, when one child was totally exhausted, Tanni would allow them to get up close to me. Not out of pity, of course; he simply didn't want to lose a drilling resource. He even let them touch me sometimes. But it was only ever a fleeting touch. All the Unearthers wanted as much of my beauty as they could get, but Tanni rationed them.

He was greedy, our Tanni. He wanted more of me than the others.

From time to time I looked at his hands. I was looking for changes, knowing any new ones would probably start with Tanni himself. What next? I wondered. Mechanically powered drills? Blades erupting from their heads? Actually, I think Tanni would have liked that. Blades. Oh yes. A development that confirmed he was turning into a weapon.

Whenever I stared at him, I found Tanni staring right back. He knew how much his direct gaze unnerved me. "I did have a question," he said one time, after I'd just spent ten minutes gasping in a side-tunnel below Second Camp. "Why do you suppose it is, Thomas, that we're the only children in Coldharbour to become Unearthers?"

I didn't answer him. I had no idea, but I didn't want him to know that. If he was unsure, let him stay that way.

"It bothers me," Tanni remarked.

"Good," I said.

Tanni smiled—as well as his stiff metal face allowed. "It doesn't matter," he said. "There are enough of us. No one else can reach down here to stop us. And if they try, I'll kill them." He said it so tonelessly that I knew he meant it. I tried to imagine what the future might be like if the new Tanni had his way. He observed me through his slits.

"We'd better not have to wait too long for the next development, Thomas."

"Is that a threat, is it?"

Tanni laughed, clamping his hand on my shoulder. "Thomas, if I was threatening you, I think you'd be sure of it. Actually, Parminder's had an idea for getting more cooperation out of you. I think it's a bit over the top, a bit overdramatic, but you know how Parminder gets."

He smiled at me and so did Parminder.

I shrugged, pretending I couldn't care less, but of course I was extremely interested in any plans Parminder might have for me.

"You remember," she said conversationally, "when you first came to Coldharbour? Do you remember telling us all about that, Thomas? You were all on your own, poor thing, and there was that warehouse, remember? The one with the wild animals, all those four-legged friends. Every night you'd end up sharing the floor with them because you couldn't shut the warehouse doors, could you?"

Parminder and Tanni left me to think about that while they went off to check the latest drilling advances. When they came back, Tanni's mood was bleak. I sensed the problem at once, because I was responsible: not enough progress; the thirsty drill-teams definitely weren't getting all the beauty Tanni thought they deserved.

It was time for Parminder's little surprise.

At first I had no idea what was happening. I was taken to a passageway. This was blocked with rock on both sides. That left me in an oblong space the size of a small bedroom. It was totally dark, and I had no idea what I was doing there. Maybe they were just going to isolate me? I told myself that, but I didn't really believe it.

I waited. I didn't know the reason why they kept me waiting at the time, but afterwards I realized it must have been because the Unearthers had to travel a long way back up to the surface to find the rats. Finally a chink of bronze light appeared in a corner of my new bedroom.

"Hi!" Parminder said cheerily. Part of her face shone through a slot about the size of a letter box. There was, in fact, a letter-box-wide slot in each of the four corners.

Parminder let the first rat in shortly afterwards.

I didn't scream. I heard it creeping around. Then it retired to the opposite corner from me and stayed there for a bit. Afterwards, it started running madly around the walls of the place, squealing, trying to find a way out. It couldn't—Parminder had closed the slot.

I think Tanni and Parminder expected me to beg at once for mercy. Or maybe they were waiting for the rat to attack me. But the rat was too afraid to do anything after they'd manhandled it down here. In any case, they were wrong if they thought they'd break me this way. I'd learned in my early Coldharbour days how to live with a rat in a room.

A second rat was let in. A third.

I moved around, made enough noise so the rats would know I was big. Once or twice their hairy bodies brushed up against me, but they always ran off again. The truth is that they must have been more scared than I was. I clung onto that knowledge. I let myself worry about the rats. Yes, that seemed like a good idea, not screaming my head off, but taking pity on the rats. "You sad sorry little squealers," I said out loud. And all the while I held onto my beauty.

After about an hour, the oxygen was almost gone. My breath became shallower and shallower, and for a while I thought me and the rats were simply going to lie down on the floor and expire together. But Tanni couldn't allow that, of course. I was dug out from the room. The rats escaped and I watched them scrambling back up a connecting tunnel.

Good luck, I thought, meaning it.

Tanni was shaking his head. Parminder no longer had any hair on the left side of her scalp.

"You are definitely the most disgustingly ugly girl I have ever seen," I told her.

"Let's kill him," she said to Tanni.

"You can't, you dope," I said. "If you do that, no more beauty! Tanni understands, even if you don't ever quite seem to get the point through that overthick skull of yours. You'd better not injure me, either," I said as she bent forward menacingly. "I haven't got much strength left. If I get any worse there won't be any beauty left, especially with Tanni taking so much." I looked directly at her. "And I'm sure you've noticed, Parminder, how much Tanni's taking for himself."

That made her think. I couldn't hurt Parminder in any other way, but at least I could do that: make her uncomfortable.

She glared at Tanni. "Is this true?"

"Shut up," he told her.

He walked up to me, tapping his metal teeth with his metal fingers.

"You know, you're right, Thomas," he said pleasantly.

"We can't do much more than we've already done to threaten you. I know you'll crack in the end, and so do you"—he gazed at me—"but to get quicker results we need to threaten someone else." He smiled. "I think I might know who, as well. In your sleep you've been muttering on and on about all your old friends. Did you know that? Helen, the twins, Walter and a little girl, Jenny. Yes, Milo's little sister. Do you know how often you've called out her name during your naps?" I wasn't aware of this, but I did know that for some reason Jenny was appearing in most of my dreams. Tanni studied me for a moment. Then he said, "Parminder thinks Jenny's dangerous, Thomas."

I said nothing.

"Parminder thinks we should kill her," Tanni said. "What do you think?"

I knew it was a mistake to say anything, but I couldn't help myself. "She's just a girl."

"Is she?" Tanni said. "Is that a fact? In that case she should be easy to kill. Unless you want to cooperate, of course. . . ."

My tongue was so dry that I had to massage my throat to get it to move. Tanni and Parminder expected me to say something. I didn't. I realized I didn't have anything to say to them. All this time I'd been worried they'd go out after the twins, Jenny, Helen, or maybe her dad, but now the threat was out in the open I knew it didn't change a thing. I couldn't give the Unearthers my beauty, no matter what they did to anyone else.

Tanni read my expression.

"You won't feel so brave about it when we have Jenny down here in front of you," he said.

"I don't want to mess around," Parminder told him. "Maybe we should just kill Jenny up there on the surface, the first chance we get. We could take one of the others prisoner. Helen, for instance. Thomas would probably react the same way if we hurt her in front of him."

"Maybe," Tanni said, not taking his eyes off me. "Anyway, she'll be easy enough to find. Thomas has already kindly let us know where they are."

"What about the giant boy who guards them?" Parminder asked.

"Walter," Tanni mused. "Twice the size of a man. Yes, he's a real danger, but what use will he be against a hundred Unearthers?"

"I don't want to send that many," Parminder protested. "It'll delay the drilling operation too long."

"We're hardly making any progress now," Tanni replied. "Thomas has made sure of that. Without more of his beauty, we could dig for hours and make no further headway."

Parminder bit her lip. "What about the mind reader, Helen? Won't she know we're coming?"

"Carnac can shield us from her."

I glared at Tanni. "Who's Carnac?" He looked back at me expressionlessly. "You stupid idiot!" I shouted at him.

"You have its name, and it's given you all this metal, but you don't even know what it is dragging you down there, do you? Tanni, listen to me. You weren't always like this. Can't you fight it? Please—"

"Who's going to lead the way back up?" Parminder asked Tanni, ignoring me totally. Her voice was hesitant. She clearly did not want to return to the surface. She only wanted the deeps of the world now.

"*We'll* lead them," Tanni told her firmly.

"What about him?" Parminder jerked her free hand at me.

"He's not going anywhere, is he. Put a guard on him."

As they strode off to make preparations, I heard Parminder say, "There's no cover of darkness for us on the surface. We're bound to be seen."

"Not until the last moment," Tanni said. "What do you think these drills are for? We'll travel underground to them. Even if they're prepared for an attack, they won't expect it from that direction."

THIRTEEN

trust

HELEN

"What is it, Helen?" Dad asked, seeing me flinch on the bed.

"Not sure. Better get dressed."

"Why?"

"Someone's coming."

I got almost no warning of the arrival of the Unearthers. I only knew they were close when startled children saw their metal heads emerge from the ground. I recognized them at once, though—these were the same steel faces Jenny had carved into Agatha.

The Unearthers arrived stealthily from several directions. Their approach was obviously planned, and they headed straight towards our shack.

Walter was the first person in our area to notice them. He always slept lightly, and though the Unearthers' voices were kept down to whispers their heavy tread across the mud woke him long before they were visible.

Who or what were they? As I dressed I nearly panicked—I couldn't read their minds! I'd grown so used to having that advantage over everyone that I immediately felt vulnerable. Something was concealing these children from me. They were like a darkness.

Dad opened the door—and recoiled in shock. I knew why. From their appearance you could barely tell the Unearthers were children at all. All that steel, all that hideous bulk, with the horror-drills attaching their bodies together. At least a hundred of them encircled the shack, but Walter made the Unearthers hesitate about getting any closer.

He stepped in front of me—and they stopped.

Without saying a word, Walter shrugged out his shoulder muscles and allowed the Unearthers to get a good long look at him—to see what a force he was. It was hard to imagine anything fazing these metal children, but when Walter towered over them they faltered.

A group of toddlers crowded around his legs, but Walter even managed to make dealing with them impressive. He motioned them back to his hut, but he took his time about it. He didn't rush, didn't do it hurriedly. Then, never taking his eyes off the Unearthers, Walter gradually raised himself to his full height, letting his arms hang loose and ready. One of the Unearthers reacted to this. She showed him her drill-hand. Walter just leveled his eyes at her; he looked straight through the girl as if she wasn't there at all. The remaining Unearthers glanced nervously at their drill-partners, no doubt wondering how they would do against him in a fight.

"Call Walter off," said a voice.

It came from a boy. He and his drill-partner stood a little apart from the rest of the Unearthers. I recognized the boy at once as the face of steel I'd seen before in Jenny's mind, the one threatening Thomas. I checked all around, but Thomas wasn't amongst them, and his mind was still blank to me. I decided not to ask about him until I knew why the Unearthers were here.

I couldn't read the mind of the boy in front of me, but I could tell that he wasn't afraid of me—or of Walter. Or, if he was, he hid his fear expertly. The girl joined at the hand with him was interesting: she made her feelings apparent, her eyes running slowly up and down my clothes as if I was a piece of filth. Dad stood alongside me, ready to intervene if he had to.

"This is Parminder," the boy said. "I'm Tanni. It doesn't matter who the others are. They follow me."

"Your dog-thing is looking at me," Parminder said, glaring at Walter. "I don't like that."

Walter didn't respond to this. Instead, he used his hands to send signals through to the children in our area, gathering them in a loose circle around the Unearthers.

"We're here if you need us," a girl called out loudly to him.

Walter gazed at Tanni as if to say, *your move*.

"Helen, is it?" Tanni remarked, disregarding him. "Oh

yes," he said, seeing my eyes widen, "Thomas told us all about you. There's nothing we don't know."

I didn't reply. I wasn't about to admit that I knew nothing about Tanni and his followers. I didn't want to give him any more of an edge than he already had.

Walter moved a step closer to my side.

"The dog's touchy when it comes to you, isn't he?" Parminder said, sizing Walter up. "Impressive, though. I've a feeling he could take out a few of the Unearthers before we finished him off. Of course, the rest of you wouldn't stand a hope."

Small flies were buzzing around Parminder's drill-parts. Attracted by the heat, I thought; the drills were still warm from use.

"What do you want?" I asked.

Tanni smiled—and I realized that I'd just demonstrated my inability to read his mind.

You stupid fool! I raged at myself.

"Oh, I don't want much at all," Tanni said smoothly. "Don't be put off by all these chunky bodies. We're only here for a talk. That's all. A little chat. Nothing more."

You liar, I thought. You're here for more than that.

"D-don't," Walter warned Parminder, as she took a pace towards me.

"Ah, so the giant s-s-speaks," she said. "Not very well, though, eh? What is he? A sort of dumb pet? I see why he keeps his mouth shut now. More effective that way."

Walter did not respond to that, but several children

near us did, closing in on the Unearthers.

Obviously annoyed with Parminder's outburst, Tanni said firmly enough for everyone to hear, "I wouldn't get too close. My lot are pretty edgy. If they feel threatened, they're likely to start up their drills." He looked at me. "We don't want anything like that happening, do we? I don't suppose Thomas, when he used his beauty to give us these bodies, ever intended them to be used against children. Let's keep it that way."

"Where is he?" I asked.

"Safe and well. Resting. The journey up from below is too hard for him to manage. He's asked to see you, though. He wants to see all his old friends."

"Does he now?" I tried to keep my expression neutral. The truth was that Tanni frightened me. He clearly knew exactly what he wanted, and I had no idea how to deal with him.

"All right," I said. "Let's talk about what Thomas wants. Go ahead."

"Not here," Tanni said. "I want some privacy. We'll go in the shack—and the giant stays outside."

"No," I answered. "He doesn't. Walter stays with us. And anything you've got to say can be said to everyone here."

Parminder smiled faintly. "Don't you trust us?"

I didn't bother to answer that.

Tanni assessed the numbers of children ranged against the Unearthers for a moment, then said, "I'll agree, on one condition. I want to see the little girl. I'd like her to join us. Where is she? Milo's sister. The one called Jenny."

None of us had expected that. Walter went unnaturally still and shook his head.

"I only want to talk with her," Tanni said.

"We're not going to harm her," Parminder added.

As soon as she said that we all knew it wasn't true. A flicker of anger crossed Tanni's face, but his poise was back in a second.

Jenny was inside Walter's hut. With a minor gesture of his hand, he motioned for a large group of teenagers to stand across the entrance. Tanni didn't try to hide his irritation this time. Any chance of getting easy access to Jenny had obviously been ruined. He dropped the casual voice. "Let me talk to Jenny," he said, "or I'll turn the Unearthers loose on everyone here. I mean it. We'll slaughter you all."

I stared at Tanni.

He stared back. "Your move," he said.

What was I supposed to do? I couldn't read the Unearthers' minds, but we had to come to some kind of decision.

Dad whispered in my ear, "Does he mean what he says?"

I nodded. You only had to look at the Unearthers' bodies to know they were capable of slaughter; they appeared to be itching to put their drills to use.

There was a noise over at Walter's hut—a teenage girl

holding Jenny back. Half in and half out of the doorway, Jenny stood in her dressing gown, watching Tanni with interest.

Dad leaned across to Walter, and said quietly, "I don't know what's going to happen, but if you had to get across there quickly and take Jenny away from the Unearthers, do you think you could do it?"

"Yes."

"Then wait for my signal."

Walter checked his distance to the hut.

"I can't d-do that and protect Helen as well."

"It's okay," I whispered. "I've got Dad."

"No." Walter shook his head. "Your Dad's not enough this time. S-stay beside me. Don't let them s-separate us."

"Do what Walter says," Dad ordered me.

Jenny peered through someone's skirted legs at Tanni. She was curious rather than afraid.

"Come here," Walter ordered her.

I understood what he was doing. He realized the teenagers wouldn't be able to protect Jenny if the Unearthers made a lunge in her direction—and he could also get away more swiftly if he already had her in his arms.

Jenny skipped lightly across the mud to be with Walter, as if everything was normal. She didn't come alone. She'd decided to bring an old friend with her—Agatha. Removing some particles of dirt off the doll's face, Jenny waved her uncertainly at all of us.

As soon as the Unearthers saw Agatha, they were transfixed. It was obvious why—Agatha was just like them. In particular, Agatha was just like Parminder. An exact likeness.

"Let me see," she rasped.

The savage appearance of the Unearthers didn't seem to bother Jenny at all. Was it because they looked like her doll, like a safe thing? She shrugged and threw Agatha at Parminder. Tanni reached out for her with his free hand, but it must have been an old instinct, because he no longer had any fingers left to catch her. Agatha clanked against his wrist. He winced, apparently worried about breaking her.

That made Jenny laugh.

"She's only a doll, stupid," she told him. "Only a doll made of stone. She can't even talk. You can't hurt her."

Walter held Jenny securely while Tanni nudged Agatha with his foot. Many of the other Unearthers crowded round him. After examining her thoroughly, he said to Jenny, "Did you make this?"

She nodded.

"Why?"

"I just did. She's a doll."

"When did you make her?"

"Before," Jenny said. "But I didn't finish her. I finished her today, but she got dirty again. Bring her. I'll show you. . . ." Since the Unearthers weren't able to pick Agatha up, Dad warily did so. Jenny took hold of Agatha, gripped her neck tightly and blew hard on her face. Some damp powdered rock fell away. Jenny casually threw the doll back at Tanni.

That's when we all saw the latest version of Agatha. She no longer had any eyes. They'd been cut out. Even Tanni frowned, seeing that. Parminder rubbed her drill-parts across the stone face. It was exactly like hers, except for the eyes.

"Is this doll meant to be me?"

Jenny shrugged.

"What do you mean by that?" Parminder growled.

Jenny shrugged again.

Tanni said, "Doesn't your doll need to see? Doesn't she need to be able to see things?"

"No." Jenny sniffed. "She doesn't care about that. She only wants to dig. See?" She put Agatha's drill hands against Walter's leg and made a *grrrrr* noise.

"But what happened to her eyes?" Tanni asked.

"Oh, she lost them," Jenny said. "They burned off one day. It was too hot. It wasn't sad. She didn't need them anymore. She's just a girl who wants to dig."

Parminder said to Tanni, "Is that what we're going to become? Are we going to end up without eyes?" She said it without emotion, as if it didn't matter to her.

"Perhaps," Tanni said. "But if so, how does the girl know?"

Jenny glanced shyly up at Parminder. "Agatha's like you, isn't she? But you're real. You're a real girl. You're not a doll. Aren't you scared about not being able to see?"

Parminder strode towards her.

Walter, in one swift movement, put the hand holding Jenny behind him and with his other hand clenched Parminder's throat. The Unearthers stirred uneasily, but Tanni ordered them to stay where they were.

"Tell this idiot to let go!" Parminder yelled. "He's choking me!"

"Shut up," Tanni said.

"What do you mean, shut up?"

Tanni wasn't listening to her. He gazed in fascination at Jenny, examining her knuckles. "Are you one of *us*?"

"No," Jenny replied.

"What then?"

Jenny rubbed Agatha's nose-slits playfully. "I'm just a girl." Then she peered inquisitively at Tanni. "Do you know where Thomas is? Do you? Helen doesn't know. Walter doesn't know. No one does. Do you know?"

"Yes, I do," Tanni said. "I know exactly where Thomas is."

Jenny immediately wriggled in Walter's arms, trying to get down.

"Take me to him!" she begged Tanni. "Oh, please take me to him! Will you? Will you?"

Tanni stared thoughtfully at Jenny. Then he faced me. "I'm leaving with this girl," he said. "If Walter or anyone else tries to stop me, I'll give an order for the Unearthers to drill into everyone. Do you understand what that means?"

Walter pushed Parminder and Tanni away, preparing to leap away with Jenny. "W-well?" he demanded, waiting for Dad's signal.

"No," I intervened. "Not yet. Not yet, Walter."

Jenny wanted to get closer to Tanni. "Let me go, Walter!" she shouted. "It's all right! Let me go! I want to go with *him*. I want to! He knows where Thomas is. He knows!"

"Jenny," Walter said, "these children d-don't want to help you find Thomas. They want something else."

"But they know where Thomas is. They said they did. They said!"

"That doesn't matter. You n-need to stay with me."

"*Let her go*," I told him.

"What?" Walter's mouth fell open. Dad was also astonished by what I'd said. Even Tanni was puzzled.

"Let her go," I repeated. "Let Jenny go with whoever she wants. Let her go with the Unearthers."

"Right, inside the shack," Dad said firmly. "Helen, Walter, Jenny, and me only. No one else. A private discussion. Walter, put a guard around the shack but come inside with us." He glanced sharply at Tanni. "I expect you to keep your people back while we're in there. Is that clear?"

Tanni pondered this a moment. "I'll give you five minutes. That's all. And I don't want any surprises." He dragged Parminder, complaining and still holding her neck, away. The rest of the Unearthers drew back. Walter placed a cordon of children around the shack before opening the door.

Once we were inside, Dad demanded, "Why, Helen? Why? I don't get it."

"Because . . ." I stopped. I didn't know, not really; I was guessing.

"You can't read their thoughts, can you?"

"No, I can't," I admitted.

"I didn't think so. So what's this about? I don't understand what you're up to. You want us to let Tanni and these Unearther-things take Jenny away? Why?"

Jenny wasn't listening. She could hardly contain her excitement at the prospect of seeing Thomas.

"That's why," I said, pointing to her with as much conviction as I could.

"Oh, come on, Helen," Dad said. "Because she *wants* to go with the Unearthers? Is that your best argument? Jenny's just a kid. You know how she's been lately. She'd go with anyone who told her they knew where to find Thomas."

"But *why*, Dad," I persisted. "That's the important question. Why does Jenny keep asking to see Thomas? There's a reason."

Walter touched my arm. He wanted to trust me. He was already attempting to see this differently, to accept the possibility of allowing Jenny to leave, but how could he? She was his world. The idea of letting her go to the Unearthers without a fight was impossible. I thought he was about to plead with me, but instead he said this:

"I can guard Jenny, but n-not if she goes with the Unearthers."

"Let her go, Walter," I said. "Please. You have to. We've got to let her get close to Thomas. There's something developing between them."

"Something worth risking Jenny's life for?" Dad asked.

I couldn't answer that for sure. My instinct told me—yes.

"Listen," Dad said. "If these metal things take Jenny underground, we won't even know where she is. If she's in trouble we won't be able to help her."

"I know."

He met my gaze. "All this on nothing more than a hunch?"

"Yes."

Jenny said, "Milo would let me go."

We all looked at her.

I said to Walter and Dad, "If Milo accepts it, will you both do the same?"

Walter checked outside, to make certain the Unearthers were keeping their distance. When he came back he wouldn't answer me.

"Another thing," I said. "I've got to go with Jenny."

"Not you." Dad waved his hand dismissively. "If we decide to let Jenny leave, we can bargain with Tanni to make sure she has company, but it'll be someone else."

"It *has* to be me," I said. "I need to know what's happening between Jenny and Thomas."

184

"We don't even know if the Unearthers are telling the truth about knowing where Thomas is!" Dad said, restraining himself from shouting.

"Yes, we do," I told him. "It was in Jenny's mind. The Unearthers are holding him underground somewhere. Actually, I don't need Jenny to show me that anymore. I'm getting a few stray thoughts from Thomas, Dad. He's in pain. Something's trying to hide him from me, but I'm finding a way through now."

Dad sighed heavily, shaking his head. "I still don't think that's a good enough argument for going with Jenny. Even if the Unearthers have Thomas, they might not let you or her see him. And perhaps it's you they want as much as Jenny." He looked at me. "Think about it: if you do this, the Unearthers will have all three of you under their control. Then they can do whatever they want, can't they? Down there, what's to prevent them?" *Getting rid of you*, he thought.

That hadn't occurred to me. If Dad was right, Jenny might never get to Thomas and I could be leading us both to our deaths.

"Let me go," I said.

"Helen . . ."

"Dad, you must. Trust me."

Walter shook his head over and over, hoping he'd misunderstood something. "Helen," he said, "w-what are you doing this for? I d-don't understand. I can l-look after Jenny. Don't you think I c-can protect her? I can, of c-course I can. If—"

"Walter . . ." I said, "please . . ."

He could easily have stopped Jenny from leaving his arms in that moment. She slipped from them into mine, and he could easily have taken her back. Instead, he let her go and followed us from the shack. Once outside, Walter peered up at Milo.

I had no idea what Milo's response would be. Jenny was his sister, and he'd been steadily watching events unfold between us and the Unearthers, but I had no idea whether he would react against Jenny leaving.

Before I lost my nerve, or Dad had time to continue the argument, I strode across the soil and said to Tanni, "You can take Jenny as long as I go with her as well. That's the deal: me and Jenny together. Or neither of us."

He shrugged, as if he didn't care, but I think he was secretly pleased.

"Where are you taking them?" Dad demanded. "I want to know where you're going before I let anyone leave."

"There aren't any street names down there," Tanni said dryly.

Dad was ready to argue forever if he had to, but I didn't give him the chance. I walked across to be next to Tanni. "Wherever we are, it doesn't matter," I said to Dad. "It won't make any difference. Don't stop us leaving."

Walter stood there, clenching and unclenching his huge hands. Every part of him was desperately forcing himself to trust me.

But he was right not to trust me completely. I'd never had any real insight into Jenny's mind. I knew now that she had predicted what was happening to the Unearthers and also the twins—and that was a gift in itself—but I sensed an additional gift in her far more important than that. Something to do with Thomas. I had to bring them together. But what if I was making a terrible mistake? I stared at Walter, knowing that, even now, if I ordered him to take Jenny from the Unearthers, he could. He could save her. There was still time. He could run faster than any of the Unearthers. They'd never catch him.

I didn't ask.

"Let's get going!" Parminder growled.

Walter and Dad glanced up at Milo. I think Walter in particular had counted on a last-minute intervention from him. When that didn't come, it took all of his effort not to snatch Jenny back.

Tanni had a last look around, and then, keeping me beside him, led the way from the shack. The rest of the Unearthers followed behind, stepping awkwardly around people for a short distance. When they came to their holes, Tanni clasped Jenny to his chest. Parminder reluctantly gripped me in the crook of her forearm. She held me harshly and gave me a warning to keep my arms tucked well inside if I didn't want them to get cut on the stone walls. There was no time for farewells.

We dropped. The last thing I saw as I arched my face towards the daylight was Walter's face.

FOURTEEN

thirst

THOMAS

While Tanni was gone, only the sound of frustrated drilling kept me going. The tone barely changed. The Unearthers hammered away, but made almost no progress.

Because I held onto my beauty. I gave them next to nothing.

I took some pride in that, but the Unearthers made me suffer for it. No food for Tommy-boy. Not a morsel. I got to be so hungry that I might have looked differently at those rats had I seen them again. But worse than the hunger was the thirst. The Unearthers didn't give me any water, and after the best part of a day without a drop mysterious things were happening to my body.

I'd stopped sweating for a start. All that heat, and not a bead. Then the itching began, a creeping itch that spread from my thighs over my whole skin, an urge to scratch that never went away. But I think what happened to my eyes scared me even more. The lids kept sticking together. I'd blink like mad to try to open them again, but that only made it worse, and I'd end up having to prise the lids apart with my fingers.

Actually, I lost it completely for a while down there. I started stumbling around Second Camp like a loon. I don't know what I hoped to find: some dampness maybe, a trickle on a wall; anything wet. The Unearthers guarding me kept a bottle of water handy as a nice tempter. "You want some of this, Thomas?" they'd say, taking the odd leisurely swig. "It's here for you. You know what you have to do to get it." It was a standoff. I withheld my beauty from them; they withheld liquid refreshment.

That little bottle of water became an object of fascination for me. I kept staring at it, and while I managed to prevent myself from begging them for some, I couldn't stand the way the level of water went down whenever the Unearthers sipped any. Eventually there was only a titchy amount left sloshing about inside. The Unearthers stayed close to the bottle, smiling away, lighting it up with their bronze faces. When only a few drips were left, one of them slowly unscrewed the cap. He tipped the bottle and, pausing for effect, dribbled the last of the water onto the cave floor.

If this was intended to drive me insane, it almost worked. It took all my self-control not to crawl over there. I kept wanting the Unearthers to look away, or do something else, so that I could go over to that patch without them seeing me. If I'd had the power in that moment to convert all of my beauty into a single mouthful of water, I'd have done it.

No respite from the heat. No relief from the dust. Tiny fine particles from the drilling kept entering my nose and mouth, and seemed to soak up any last dregs of moisture I might have inside. Actually, as my body dried out the effects were really bizarre. First my joints seized up, making any movement excruciatingly painful. Next my lips blistered; then, when I felt my hair, it was as dry as wire. At some point I stopped being able to move my tongue properly. It felt like a rough wooden stake stuffed in my throat. And then this happened—my face contracted. That was definitely the most alarming thing of all, prodding my face and feeling the skin give way, the looseness of the dried-up skin against the bones beneath.

No weeping, of course. No tears. Insufficient moisture left for those. Not that I'd have given the Unearthers the satisfaction of seeing them anyway. From time to time I drifted into a delirious state. During those times I was aware of saying things to myself, gabbling on, but my throat was so stripped it came out like someone else's weird croak. A bit later the pain of swallowing became more than I could bear, and I stopped talking altogether.

But you know something, I put up with it. The more time I spent with the Unearthers the more certain I was that whatever possessed them was nothing my beauty was ever intended to help. I focused on that, and tried to ignore the deterioration of my body. No point thinking about what kind of state I was in. It was obvious that the Unearthers weren't going to give me any of my beauty back. They weren't like Milo. No, they'd take it all, squeeze out what they could until I was dead. After that, they'd probably use my dried-out bones as something to rest their freakish bodies against.

I got consolation from one thing, though: listening to the feeble noise coming from the drill-face. The Unearthers weren't getting anywhere. Some trickles of my beauty escaped—I couldn't stop the Unearthers using their drills altogether—but at least they weren't making any new progress.

A few more hours passed, and my body decided to give me an additional bit of good news: I no longer felt hungry. It was as if my stomach had shut down. That made sense—no juices left to digest the food with. What about my blood? I could almost feel it thickening, my heart struggling to stir it around.

Finally even my guards started getting anxious.

"When's Tanni coming back?" one said. "Maybe we should give the prisoner a drink. I don't want him collapsing on us. Even if his throat's closed up, we could force it down."

"Tanni'll murder us if we make it easier on him."

"He'll murder us if he dies as well."

Tanni. I hadn't thought about him for a while, but as my body collapsed I found myself increasingly dreading his return. It was mad, really. You'd think I'd have been more worried about whether I got out of this alive, but I'd come this far, and didn't think about my own death as much as I expected. No, what I truly feared, dreaded with all my heart, was Tanni showing up with an inventive new way to make me give up my beauty. Because if anyone could do it, it was him. The possibility terrified me. I'd endured for so long already that the thought of becoming pathetic, of giving up now, or of having the beauty somehow tricked out of me, was unbearable.

What about death, though? I did think about that sometimes too. I even found a bright side. If I died my beauty went with me, at least. That way the Unearthers would never get what they wanted. They'd be stuck, bitter and useless, at the drill-head forever.

But I didn't want to die. Not really. I wasn't ready for that. I wanted to live. Even in my weakened state, I couldn't pretend otherwise. And I clung onto a shred of hope that came from an unexpected place.

Jenny.

She wasn't just an occasional dream anymore. She dominated my every thought. What was it about her? From the first moment she'd arrived in Coldharbour, I'd been drawn in some way to that young girl. The Unearthers had distracted me, using my beauty for a purpose it was never meant for. But a part of my beauty still wanted to be closer to Jenny. Thinking about her made me feel frightened, excited, humble even. And there was something else: whenever I thought about Jenny, didn't the sound of the Roar increase almost imperceptibly? Didn't its tone change, as if it might be afraid?

I felt sure it did. I focused on taking a little pleasure from that.

Then Tanni and my favorite girl Parminder returned.

Tanni didn't tell me that he had Jenny and Helen at first. Instead, he came straight over and offered me a fresh drink of cold water. I hated him for that. "No beauty strings attached," he said. "Just take it."

I nearly did, too. When he held it out, dangling a full bottle in front of me, and all I had to do was reach out a hand for it, I almost did. I would have done if he hadn't wanted me to so much.

"Get your strength back," he said. "Get that beauty flowing like it used to."

"No," I said.

"No? Have you seen what you look like? Take a drink."

I didn't bother saying anything else; my throat hurt too much to waste words.

Tanni slurped from the bottle, eyeing me contemplatively.

"We've captured Helen and Jenny now," he said. "Parminder wants to bring them straight down and threaten them in front of you. She thinks you'll cooperate fast enough then."

He watched my reaction to that, and then got up. I

expected him to haul the girls down at once, but he didn't. Instead, he spent the next hour or so in the upper tunnels where Jenny and Helen were being kept. I knew from his conversations with Parminder that he'd prefer them deeper, but Jenny couldn't stand the dry stale air of Base Camp, and for some reason Tanni seemed anxious to keep her happy. So he isolated her in a tunnel near the surface. I don't think he was particularly interested in Helen. It was Jenny who intrigued him. He'd even had one of the Unearthers go back to the surface and find a flashlight, because she cried out for more light.

Helen, I thought, can you hear me? Do you know what's happening down here?

Parminder wanted to scare the life out of me the second she got back from the fresh air of Coldharbour, but Tanni was in less of a hurry. Jenny bothered him. Like me, he understood that there was an unusual quality about her, but he didn't know what it was. That in itself disturbed me. Whenever Tanni took an interest in someone, he normally found a way to get to them.

"Jenny's dangerous, not useful that I can see," Parminder said to him, when they were back in Second Camp. "That doll she made's mesmerized you. Get over it. We need to find a way to restart the drilling."

Tanni ignored Parminder's comments, and kept forcing her to go back up to where they were keeping the girls. Each time he returned he seemed more mystified and troubled than ever.

Good. I liked to see Tanni suffering.

But I had to find a way to reach Jenny myself. How could I do that? I couldn't ask Tanni to let me see her. If he saw that I wanted to, he'd be suspicious at once. So don't ask, I thought. Do the opposite. Tanni's always searching for a weakness in you. Give him one. Give him what he wants to see.

I couldn't come out with it in one go—I had to be careful, reveal it in dribs and drabs; a small hint here, a cringe there. I was so exhausted I had no idea if my plan was working, but perhaps that very exhaustion helped persuade Tanni.

I pretended that I was *terrified* of Jenny. I winced whenever he mentioned her name. I waited until, observing me carefully, he suggested I should meet her—and reacted with horror. Parminder took the bait soon enough, but Tanni remained dubious, and I thought I'd never be able to keep up the pretense. Finally, though, after Tanni returned yet again from seeing Jenny, you could see that he and Parminder had had a furious argument.

"All right," he said to her. "Let's do it."

Without further discussion an arm scooped me up and dragged me out of Second Camp. Parminder did the dragging—her speciality. I guessed where I was being taken and screamed as well as my throat allowed.

Helen, I thought, I'm depending on you now. Help me make this convincing.

It was a long way up to the cell. A single tunnel dug from below and not accessible from above led there, so there was no chance of escape to the surface. I was pulled into the cell and dumped on the floor. The flashlight beam shone into my eyes, so at first I could only see the girls' silhouettes. I wanted to go straight over to Jenny, but with Tanni watching me closely I had to continue the charade. I backed away, scrambling on my knees to the rear of the cave. Helen did the rest.

"Get Thomas away from us!" she shrieked, hiding Jenny behind her. "Get him out of here!"

From my place squeezed against the cave wall I took the risk of glancing up to see Jenny. I expected her to look different, somehow, but she didn't. There she was, the same serious-faced girl I remembered. My extreme reaction to her presence completely bewildered her, of course. From behind Helen's back she reached out a hand to me.

"Don't touch him!" Helen shouted at the top of her voice.

I shrank against the wall, while Jenny tried to squirm from Helen's grasp. I held Parminder's foot, whining and begging for her protection. "Get off!" she said. In disgust she kicked me away.

At the same moment Helen let go of Jenny.

We arrived together near the middle of the cave.

I had a strong urge to put my hands on her, but Tanni was watching me and I resisted it.

"What's the matter?" Jenny asked, still upset by how I'd

reacted. "I won't hurt you. I like you. Why are you shout-ing?" She reached out to touch my face, and I let her. I don't know what I expected to feel: a spark; a flash; some-thing my beauty recognized at least.

But I felt—nothing. Nothing. How could it be nothing?

I studied Jenny, wondering if *she* might look different. But there was no change there either, just an anxious smile. Helen glanced at me uncertainly. Clearly, she'd also expected more.

"Not so afraid of Jenny now, Thomas, I see," Tanni noted. "I don't think you've been entirely honest with us, have you?"

"This has all been a complete waste of time!" Parmin-der snarled. "We've waited hours, and this is the result! Thomas won't give us his beauty unless we punish them. We should have done that from the beginning." She appraised both girls, selecting between them, and lifted her drill-hand.

"No!" Helen yelled, putting herself in front of Jenny.

Parminder pushed Helen aside, her drills angling towards Jenny's face.

Then Tanni's free hand shot out. He held Parminder back.

And do you know something: even then, even after everything that had happened, I still had a sliver of faith in Tanni. For a moment I believed he'd raised that hand to stop Parminder, and everything might be different, because if Tanni wanted it to be different, I knew it still could be.

"Not Jenny," he said. "No. I'm still interested in her. Use the edge of the drill on Helen first."

This time it was me who stood shakily between Parminder and Helen.

Helen glared fiercely at me. "They're just after your beauty! Don't give them it! Don't give them *anything* because of me! Do you hear, Thomas? Are you listening?" She gripped my arm. "Do you know what's down there, under the earth, waiting for the Unearthers? An offspring of—"

Parminder knocked Helen across the cell. Her head clattered against the rock wall, leaving her dazed.

"Don't hurt her," I shouted.

Tanni grabbed me. "And in return you'll do what, Thomas?"

"I . . . I'll . . ." I stared at him. "Leave them both alone and I'll give you all the beauty you need."

FIFTEEN

second skin

HELEN

"Helen! They hurt you!"

Jenny cupped my face in the hollow of her hands, helping me up. I staggered to my feet. Luckily only the outside of Parminder's drill-hand had struck me. No broken bones.

With my head spinning, I watched Thomas being hauled across the floor.

You could see that Parminder liked doing that, bumping him along, his face banging off the stone. From Thomas's thoughts, coming through clearly now, I knew Parminder hadn't always been this way. At the beginning, she'd been as terrified as any of the Unearthers by the stiffening feel in her belly as the steel took control.

I might have liked that earlier Parminder. No one could like her now. Carnac, firstborn of the Roar, totally controlled her actions. He dominated her, and Parminder lugged poor Thomas across the cave as if he was nothing more than a carcass.

The three of them dropped down the tunnel-chute.

It was such a relief to be in contact with Thomas's thoughts again—I'd worked endlessly on breaking Carnac's barrier to his mind—but seeing him was almost unbearable. The things the Unearthers had done to him! I'd expected Thomas to look bad when he was thrown onto the floor, but not this bad: eyelids matted with gunk, his lips broken, a livid red face shriveled up like a geriatric's.

As the Unearthers carried him away, he looked quickly at me across the floor of the cave, then he was gone. Down the tunnel-chute Thomas sped, a familiar motion to him now, with the heat of the deeps rising up and Parminder holding his neck an inch short of breaking.

Escape, he thought. Are you listening, Helen?

I was listening, but I didn't know how. Escape from this place? The only way out was the same way Thomas had gone, and that drop-chute fed down, not towards the surface.

"No, no," Jenny said, standing up in alarm and waving her arms.

It was the flashlight. The batteries were already low when Tanni brought it to us, and now they were almost gone. We'd be in total darkness soon. I tried to recall if flashlights petered out gradually or instantly.

"Oh, what happened between you?" I said to Jenny. "What *didn't* happen?"

She gazed at me sadly. "I'm sorry."

She had no idea what was supposed to have taken place between herself and Thomas. They'd both wanted to meet. They'd both yearned for it. Thomas would have let Parminder tear his hand off, if he could first have touched Jenny, he felt so strongly that he had to.

How could nothing have happened?

Jenny blinked in the last of the light.

"Where's Walter?" She tried to rub the dirt off her hands. "He's mad at me, isn't he? He thinks I've left him behind."

"No, he doesn't. Of course not. The tunnels are too small for him to get down, that's all."

"Tanni wants to hurt me now," Jenny said.

I hesitated. How much should I tell her?

And then Jenny said this: "We're going to die down here, aren't we?"

I peered at the face now only barely lit by the flashlight.

"No, we're not," I told her. We are *not* going to die. We're going to get out of here."

"How?"

"I . . ."

Jenny lifted her hand to rub her brow, then stopped.

Something thin, like a piece of white string, dangled from her palm. At first I thought it must be fibers of her dressing gown come loose, but as Jenny raised her hand the substance stretched like elastic.

"It's sticky," she said. "Like goo."

A chill ran through me, but Jenny didn't seem concerned. She opened out her fingers and more of the sticky white substance oozed out. It came from four enlarged pores in the middle of both her hands.

"Jenny, do you know what this is?"

"No." Her expression was inquisitive, not afraid. "Look," she said. Taking off her shoes and socks, she attached one of the sticky white strands to her bare left foot. "I'm a spider," she said. "Is that what I am?"

"I don't know. Do you . . . *want* to be a spider?"

"No. But I can do things." She showed me: she pressed the area around the pores with her thumbs, making the substance flow more freely. It seeped out of the center of both her hands, a thick white gummy paste. "Watch," Jenny said. She dabbed her face—two blobs on her cheeks. Then she wiped the paste over the upper half of her forehead and without pausing drew her hands over the entire length of her hair. In the faint light of the cave it shone slickly.

"What are you doing, Jenny?"

"I'm just playing," she said. "Do you want some?" She opened her hand and I dipped my fingers into the paste. It did not adhere to me. It remained on Jenny. She shrugged, rubbing some more on her face.

Then she covered part of her mouth.

I wanted to grab her hands when I saw that, but I didn't know if I should.

"Jenny, what are you doing?"

"I'm just playing." She coated the underside of her arms. She dabbed her nose and sniffed. She stuck out her tongue and licked the paste. "Ugh!" she said.

"What does it taste like?"

"It tastes funny."

"Are you supposed to eat it?"

"No." Jenny giggled. "Don't be silly." She continued to wipe her hands across her body. Then she quickly took off all her clothes down to her underwear and rubbed the paste over her tummy and legs and back. She moved faster and faster. Half of her was now coated in the substance.

I didn't know what to do. Grab her arms? Hold her back? I wanted to protect her somehow, at least slow her down, but I didn't know if I should. I didn't understand what was taking place.

"Jenny—"

"It's all right. I'm only playing."

"Is it because of what Thomas did? When you touched him, I mean?"

"I don't know. He was angry with me."

"No, he only seemed that way."

"He ran away from me."

Jenny carried on sliding her hands over her body, squeezing her palms when the paste would not come out fast enough. The middle of her back was a problem. She couldn't reach it. For a moment that held her up. Then she squeezed a large amount of paste on the floor and rolled her back in it. I would have stopped her if she'd shown any sign of being afraid.

Both Jenny's legs were now fully coated. She put them together and crossed her ankles, spreading the paste thoroughly until there was only the shape of a single broad white leg. She smiled at me. Moving her arms restlessly, she completed her neck and shoulders. Then she arrived at her eyes. I thought she might stop there, but she didn't. She shut the lids and sealed them up with the paste.

"Wait," I said, grabbing her hand.

"It's all right, Helen."

I noticed her eyeballs still flickering about under the whiteness covering them.

"Can you see me, Jenny?"

"No."

"Don't you mind?"

"No." Her hands moved rapidly. She covered her nose, both little nostrils. Then she closed her lips and did her mouth. For a moment she struggled to breathe.

"Jenny?"

She'd stopped breathing altogether. She sat there, her body upright, not breathing.

"Jenny?" I scraped frantically at her lips, but the substance would not budge. It was tight over her whole face, already as hard and smooth as plastic. "Jenny! Can you hear me?"

Her head nodded slightly. There was a small patch of skin still showing under her left ear. She rubbed a finger across it. After that she stopped moving altogether. She was entirely covered in paste. Her body was white and smoothly glistening. Her hair lay flattened against her scalp. I listened to her chest to see if I could still hear her heart. Yes. A tiny beat.

"Jenny?" Nothing this time. "Jenny, please say something."

Silence. I tapped her arm, and it was like tapping glass.

Would she be as brittle as glass?

As delicately as possible, I laid her down on her side. She rested there, unmoving, like a plastic mold of a girl, her legs tight together, one arm laid down the side of her body, the other lifted to her ear, the last place she had put her hand. Her mind was empty.

"Jenny?"

No response. Nearby, the light from the flashlight beam was virtually gone, but it hardly mattered—the new Jenny radiated her own pale light. She shone. I examined her, touching the glimmering membrane in several places. It didn't feel like glass or plastic. It was more delicate. Like a second skin. Smooth and warm. Her heart beat only slowly, but it did beat. Jenny was still alive, somewhere inside there.

What was happening? Was this extra hard skin some kind of protection? Some kind of shell in which to hibernate? A cocoon? Like the chrysalis of a caterpillar? As soon as I thought that, I felt a warning. It came from my own mind.

The Roar.

She was there. All this time she and her newborn had been hiding in the tangles of my thoughts, quietly eavesdropping.

And under me, quietly communicating with her, I now registered another presence: Carnac. He no longer bothered to conceal himself from me. There he was, the Roar's offspring, sliding and slipping about in the molten core. All his focus was bent on one thing: bringing the Unearthers down to him. I sensed his frustration at the way Thomas continued to withhold his beauty, but Carnac felt more confident now—confident enough to show his presence to me. He called out and the Roar answered him. She let him know how close she was.

I wrenched my mind away from them.

Below us, Thomas was still descending, being taken down to the drill-depths. He had no intention of giving the Unearthers anything, of course. He'd only pretended to submit, knowing what Parminder and Tanni would do to Jenny and me otherwise. As Parminder hauled him below Second Camp, Thomas attempted to come up with delaying tactics.

Helen, he thought, do you know what's going to happen when the Unearthers realize that I won't give them any beauty? Get out. Get out now. I'll give you as much time as I can.

I shuffled across the cell floor, pulling Jenny along by her joined ankles. The drop-chute fell blackly under us.

Would Jenny survive the journey? Her cocoon or what-ever it was might shatter at the first bump. No choices left. I'd have to take that risk, but I wanted to give her shell a chance to harden first.

To remove the rest of the Unearthers from the upper tunnels, Thomas said to Tanni, "I need all of you in one location for the beauty to work."

"Why?"

"It's the only way I can release it in the way you need. Second Camp will do."

Seeing the behavior of the Unearthers through Thomas's eyes, I could tell that Tanni was suspicious. His patience had almost snapped. Thomas, though, by tempting him with the final prize of his beauty, thought he could count on his grudging cooperation for a little longer. If Thomas didn't give up all his beauty after that, he knew that Parminder would probably get to do what-ever she liked with him.

"I'm not in a fit state," Thomas said, as the Unearthers gathered. "Thanks to the way you've treated me, I'm a wreck. Get me some food, and something to flipping keep me cool, and a drink. Get me a drink!"

"Give him nothing," said Parminder.

Tanni gestured for a dribble of water to be provided. "Disgusting," Thomas protested, but he didn't spit it out. "I'm too hot!" he said. "Cool me down. I'm sick of this heat! *Cool me down*!" Tanni twitched with irritation, but ordered an Unearther to run a dirty edge of cloth against a moist wall. Thomas snatched up the cloth himself and, while he rubbed it over his head, thought about Jenny. How could nothing have happened between them?

You're wrong, Thomas, I thought, knowing he couldn't hear me. You're wrong.

"Food," he croaked. "Get me food. I need it."

Tanni was seething with impatience. He offered Thomas a handful of food—something so putrid that he couldn't identify it. "More water," Thomas insisted, chewing it slowly. "I can't get this stinking stuff down my throat, you know that."

"Eat it or don't," Tanni said. He raised a hairless eyebrow. "Are you lying to us, Thomas? Is that what you're doing? Is that what all this is about? Playing for time? Stalling? Better not be. You know what I'll do to you if you are."

I positioned Jenny over the edge of the drop-chute. Should she be above or below me? If I put her below, I might crush her when we landed. Best if I went first, backwards, with Jenny in my arms.

I gathered her up and leaned over the rim.

"Well?" Tanni demanded. "We're waiting."

"It's not a simple thing," Thomas said. "You don't know anything about how my beauty works, so shut up." He closed his eyes, pretending to concentrate. "Everyone stop fidgeting with your drills," he said. "I need complete quiet." He got it, too. For the first time since the Unearthers acquired their drills they put them by their sides, not fiddling with them. Silence in Second Camp.

"Well?" Tanni said, placing his free arm on Thomas's neck.

"Take your hand off me. Did you hear? Take it off!"

Tanni reluctantly did so and afterwards Thomas stood there, surrounded by the massed bodies of all the Unearthers. He just stood there. He'd run out of ideas for delaying things further; or rather, he was too tired to come up with any more. He slumped quietly down on the hot floor of the cave. With his eyes closed, he stayed that way for as long as he could, thinking, Helen, if you're not already gone—now.

Clutching Jenny, I dropped over the rim of the chute.

We fell—a terrible few seconds where I experienced nothing but air. Then an inclined slope picked us up and I pressed my back into it, holding Jenny tightly. The tunnel wasn't entirely smooth. Where the Unearthers had altered their drilling actions on the way down there were small sharp ridges. My spine hit every one of them. At one point I thought my back had snapped and I screamed out.

No Unearthers to hear me, of course. Thomas had made sure of that.

"Our drills aren't improving," Parminder hissed at Tanni. "He's lying. It's obvious. I told you he would!"

"You have to be patient," Thomas told her. "Give me a moment."

"You're holding back," Tanni said.

"I'm not."

"Yes, you are, Thomas. Even more than before, if anything. Do you think I don't know that? What are you hoping to achieve? What—" He glanced sharply at a large pair of Unearthers. "Make sure the prisoners are still in the cell!"

SIXTEEN

the protector

DAD

I'd let Helen go. Without lifting a finger to prevent it, I'd let the Unearthers take my daughter and Jenny away. It had seemed the right thing to do at the time. I did it because Helen asked me to, because I trusted her, and because when she said there was no other way I believed her.

But I'd allowed her to rush me into a decision.

Was that the action of a good father? I'm sure all parents doubted themselves when they saw their children fleeing from home the moment Milo appeared in the sky—but none of those parents had left their children in the hands of the Unearthers.

If anything, Walter blamed himself more than I did. They'd all gone from him now, I realized: the whole original first generation Milo had commanded him to protect— Thomas, Helen, the twins and Jenny; all of them.

And he couldn't bear it. After Jenny's waving hand disappeared, he spent hours examining the drop-tunnel, trying to find a way down. His size was suddenly a curse. Afterwards, he strode half out of his mind across Cold-harbour, questioning everyone until, in the northwest, he discovered the drilling holes made by the Unearthers.

We couldn't be sure the girls would be taken there, but we had no better information to go on, and so decided to head that way. What to do when we arrived, though? There was no machinery in Coldharbour that could dig to the bottom of those holes, even if we knew which ones to choose. Someone wondered if we might flush the Unearthers out by piping seawater down them, but, even if we could obtain the equipment, flushing would be more likely to drown Helen and Jenny than get them safely out.

"Give the word," a teenage girl said to Walter, "and we'll go down the holes ourselves. There are plenty of us willing to volunteer, if you ask."

Walter raised his sunken head and I understood some-thing: if he'd spoken up then, if he had simply requested it, every single one of the kids around us would have gone without complaint into those dark shafts.

But before Walter could make any kind of decision, a noise shook us. Milo's voice. It was so loud that for a moment I thought the Roar must have penetrated his defense, and we'd look up to see his wings breaking apart in the sky.

"THERE ARE CHILDREN DROWNING," he called. "CHILDREN ARE DROWNING AT THE

SOUTHEASTERN BORDER OF COLDHAR-
BOUR! I WILL ELEVATE A WING. ONCE I DO SO
THE ROAR WILL TAKE AS MANY AS IT CAN.
THOSE OF YOU ON THE SOUTHEASTERN
COASTLINE MOVE AWAY FROM THE SEA. CHIL-
DREN ARE DROWNING. . . ."

"I don't understand," a boy said, as Milo repeated the
message. "What's at the southeastern border?"

"The ocean," I said.

And then Walter and I said it together: "The twins."

"Take me with you," I demanded. Knowing how much
faster he could run than me, I latched onto his shoulder
and hung on grimly. I'd never seen Walter move like he
did now. His strides hardly touched the mud. Within
minutes the ocean was in view, and we were crashing
towards it. All the children in the area were rushing past
us, trying to get as far from the beach as they could. As we
neared it, Milo issued a second warning:

"THOSE STILL CLOSE TO THE SHORELINE
SECURE YOURSELVES! SECURE YOURSELVES! I
AM LIFTING A WING. IT WILL ONLY BE FOR A
BRIEF TIME. DO NOT BE AFRAID."

A grinding noise followed, the sound of Milo's wing
tips being torn loose from the seabed. At the same
moment the usual pounding on that part of his wing
became a hailstorm—the Roar, I thought, aware of
events, seeking its opportunity.

Walter covered the last distance to the sea in three

enormous strides. Leaping straight over the now-deserted beach, he landed in the surf and waded out. Milo's wing was raised. In the narrow gap between it and the waves was a glimmer of sunshine. Into that gap came a power that brought a spray off the sea as it hunted across the water.

Shielding me behind his back, Walter strode out. "Emily! F-Freda!" The waves, given impetus by the Roar, smashed into his face, but he ignored them. "Where are you? C-come to me! Come to me!"

A frail scream from my left.

"Walts!" A wrist broke the water, then fell back under. Walter plunged beneath the waves. And then he had her in his arms—Freda, her face wild. There was no sign of Emily.

"Find her!" she shrieked. "Find . . . find her, Walts!" Freda was so weak that she could barely talk. "There!" she wailed, water dribbling from her mouth. "Emms was there! I 'ad her, but . . . I couldn't hold on! Walts, I 'ad her in my hand! Just now I did!" She dipped her face in the water, choking immediately.

"Give Freda over to me," I said.

Walter handed her across, took a lungful of air, and dived for Emily. For over a minute there was no sign of him. Then he emerged, empty-handed. He took another huge breath and went back under: rose, dived, rose, dived, tirelessly.

Freda was shaking in my arms. Her head lolled from side to side, her arms still paddling the waves, as if she'd been doing that for so long she couldn't stop.

Walter emerged again, and this time there was a shape in his arms.

"Emms!" Freda squealed.

A cry of triumph came from the shore as thousands of distant children saw that Walter held a girl. At the same time Milo brought his wing down with a crash and the wind seeking out the children ended.

With Freda clutching me, I reached the shallows and ran across the sand. Walter had already laid Emily carefully down, and now he was frantic, unsure whether to place her on her back or her front. She wasn't moving.

I had no proper medical training. All I knew about helping victims of drowning came from a basic-level first-aid course I'd taken over twenty years earlier. I tried to remember it. Check her pulse, I thought. How? I felt her wrist, then remembered a better place: the carotid artery in her neck. I put my fingers there. Nothing.

"I'm going to breathe for her," I told Walter. "I need your help. You're going to have to massage her heart." I took his hand and placed it at the sternum under Emily's ribs, showing him what to do. "Thrust hard, pressing up, towards her chest. Here. Like this. Wait until I've done my breaths. Do you understand?" He nodded, but I could see he was hesitant about using his big thumbs. "If you crack her ribs it doesn't matter," I told him. "They"ll mend. She'll die if we don't get her heart started quickly."

I took a steadying breath of my own. I had to keep

myself calm, otherwise I wouldn't be able to do this properly. Pinching Emily's nostrils, I tilted back her head. Then I put my mouth over hers. Her lips were so cold. Slowly I breathed air into her while Walter, following my instructions, used his thumbs. He pushed down rhythmically: fifteen times to my two breaths, fifteen times to my two breaths, fifteen times to my two breaths.

A minute went by.

"Don't stop!" Freda shrieked.

Walter studied me closely, his thumbs staying to my rhythm, while Emily's chest mechanically rose and fell.

Out of the corner of my eye, I saw a far-off child shaking her head.

"Keep going!" Freda said. "Walter, do yer hear me? Don't you dare stop! Don't you dare!"

Another thirty seconds. Another. Emily was lifeless under us. Yet another thirty seconds and now Walter was crying. Apart from that it was entirely silent on the beach. Walter kept pushing in his thumbs, pushing in his thumbs.

And then Emily's body jackknifed. She convulsed under me, seawater shooting from her mouth. I pulled back from her lips and as I did she let out a scream that went on and on and made her whole body shake.

"Emms! Emms!" Freda said.

Emily took a few ragged gasps, coughed out more seawater, and then fell back exhausted. I placed her in the recovery position, as well as I remembered it, laying her on her side. For a time she stayed almost entirely still, trickles of water spilling from the corners of her blanched lips, not sure where she was. Then she saw Walter.

"Oh," she murmured, reaching for his hands.

We waited on the beach. Only when I decided that Emily was well enough to be moved did I ask Walter to pick her up. He crouched down, placed both girls carefully on his shoulders and set off. I followed behind. Emily twisted around every few seconds, staring mournfully back at the sea.

When we arrived back neither girl was strong enough to make her own way into the shack, so Walter carried them in, placing them together on their mattress.

"Where yer going?" Emily asked, clutching at him when he tried to leave.

"Only b-be a moment," he said. He left, returning with bundles of dry clothing. Together we helped the twins remove their sodden dresses and change into the new clothes. In an attempt to get warm, the girls put on virtually everything Walter offered, including scarves and jumpers that reached below their knees. "You look f-fine in those," Walter said. "Here." He held out some food, but the girls were too exhausted to eat.

"Later," Emily said, gazing sharply round. "Where're Helen and Jenny?"

Walter told them, and both girls shrank back into their blankets.

"We got news of our own," Freda said, gazing at us both.

I knew that half the neighborhood was camped outside our shack, waiting for that news. Everyone understood the importance of Emily and Freda's journey to the sea. The longer they'd been away the less likely it seemed we would ever know if the rumor about something wonderful down there was true. But all the children had clung to that hope anyway, because what else did they have to cling to?

"We found it," Emily whispered.

"The Protector?" I asked.

She nodded tightly. "It's sealed in. It can't get away from the bottom. All these years fishes 'ave been gnawing at it, not even knowing what it was, thinking it's food. We saw where their mouths 'ad been." She suddenly wept, and Freda put her arm around her.

"We tried to free it," Freda sobbed, "but how? How could we? There was just uz two. We weren't enough. We could only free the mud off its eye. Only one eye. That's all we found. All this time, and that's all we could do! If Emms hadn't pulled uz away when she did, we'd never 'ave even made it back."

Both girls clasped each other.

"We didn't want to leave it there. Not on its own," Freda murmured.

Emily lifted her hand to Walter's lips. "You saved me, lovely boy," she told him, "but you can't stay 'ere. You got to find Jenny and Thomas. It all depends on you now. Find 'em, Walts."

We departed for western Coldharbour less than an hour later.

The twins didn't want to be a burden to Walter, and insisted on being left behind, but he refused to let them, and they were too tired to argue against him for long. I was nervous, because we had no real plan. Our only clear objective was to reach the area the Unearthers appeared to have made their base. Hundreds of additional children joined us on the journey, principally Walter's visitors and other toddlers who recognized him. Walter let them trail along. It was evident that danger could come from any direction now, and he didn't want to leave them without protection.

"Weapons?" someone asked at one point. "You saw those drills."

A good question. What weapons did we have that would be effective against the Unearthers' steel skeletons? None. Well, that wasn't quite true. We had one weapon— Walter. Who else could physically stand up to the Unearthers? As we set off, I think Walter realized this too, and throughout the long northwestward journey he became increasingly withdrawn. Small children crowded around his legs, but he paid them scant attention. He only spoke once in a while to see how the twins were doing.

Emily rested on Walter's left shoulder, the place Jenny had always been most comfortable. Freda, slightly stronger, nestled against his right arm. From time to time a youngster would sneak up his legs and perch on his body, but Walter hardly seemed aware of them. His mind was obviously set on other affairs. As I watched him, his expression barely changed. He kept his eyes fixed on the horizon, his tread neither fast nor slow, as if he was pacing himself, minding his strength.

We moved rapidly across Coldharbour, with runners going ahead to ensure a clear passage. Once I caught Walter rippling his back, thoroughly loosening out the muscles of his shoulders. Even under his patchwork jacket, you could tell the power there. He'd never truly used his muscles before, never really tested them. Some people thought that carrying doors and similar objects in errands across Coldharbour must be an effort for him, but I could tell he hardly felt their weight. As I studied Walter now, his arms poised, the huge wrists held relaxed and ready, I knew why I'd seen fear in the eyes of Unearthers when he stood before them outside the shack.

The twins, ill as they were, noticed Walter's grim, unchanging expression. Emily tugged at him. When Walter didn't respond, she murmured in his ear, "Take care, you wonder."

I don't think he even heard.

SEVENTEEN

the weight of a child

HELEN

The drop-chute never seemed to come to an end.

What was I going to do? Even if Jenny and I landed safely, I had no idea how to get back to the surface. Every inch downward was one I'd have to climb back, a step at a time. How would I be able to do that with Jenny's full weight in my arms?

I knew something with absolute certainty: if the Unearthers found us, they'd kill us. I'm not sure when I knew it. Maybe it was when Jenny went into her cocoon and Carnac finally lowered his guard. Maybe it was the Unearthers' treatment of Thomas, or the way Parminder had slapped me against the wall. Whatever the reason, it made me desperate to wake Jenny.

The drop-chute dumped us inside a small cave. As I struck the floor Jenny slipped from my arms, striking the wall. I winced, but her cocoon wasn't fractured.

You tough little girl, I thought. What's happening to

you inside there?

The cave was empty, but I understood from Thomas that the Unearthers were already spreading out from Second Camp—and they knew exactly where to find us.

Jenny's second skin illuminated five upward-pointing tunnels leading from the cave. Four were too steep to walk up. One was just possible if I didn't have to carry Jenny too far. I picked Jenny up in both arms and started along the tunnel. After less than five minutes I was exhausted. The tunnel was dry, hot, and nearly airless, with Jenny like a dead weight in my hands. I had to shift her constantly, resting different muscles in my back.

Then, below me, I felt swift movements in the tunnels—the first of the Unearthers closing in. Dozens were traveling at great speed, working their way methodically up the main connecting passageways.

Thomas was still helping me. Dragged by Parminder, with what little energy he had left he kicked out at her. I tried to speed up, but it only exhausted me sooner. Several times I fell to my knees. "Wake up, Jenny," I said. "You have to."

When she became too heavy to carry, I put her on the floor of the passage and pulled her along by her ankles. Beneath me, Tanni had reached the small cave we'd set off from. Unhesitatingly he and six other pairs of Unearthers went up the correct tunnel.

He chose this moment to open up his mind. All this time Carnac had shielded the Unearthers from me, but now he let Tanni deliver a message.

"You'll never make it," Tanni thought. "Give up and I'll spare you. I'll spare Jenny as well. I promise. There's no chance of reaching the surface in time. Not before we overtake you. And even if you do, others will be waiting there. I've sent them ahead."

That part was the truth; the first thing he'd said was a lie.

I came to a place where the passage split into three more. The main passage went on as before, only slightly easier. I was tempted. The most difficult, narrower tunnel went almost straight up. I couldn't carry Jenny in my arms that way. Tanni, of course, realized that too.

I loosened the leather belt of my jeans. How strong was it? Wrapping it around Jenny's back and under the cleft of her arm, I tested her weight. It didn't snap. I fastened the buckle strap over my head, gradually letting go of Jenny's body until she swung against me. The heaviness was shocking, all the pressure on my neck, but at least my hands were free now.

The Unearther drills had left small notches in the tunnel walls—just enough to get a toe or finger hold into. I put my left foot, my strongest, on one such hold, and reached up for a crack above with my fingernails. It was agony moving like this, the process painfully slow, especially if I paused for a rest, so I tried to establish a rhythm.

Keep going, I thought. Keep on the move.

After only a few minutes, I was weeping from the pain

in my neck. Tanni passed by the branching point below me, and though he paused for a moment to consider the tunnel I'd chosen, he and the rest of the Unearthers pressed on up the main passage.

Shortly afterwards I came to a small side tunnel. I rested there for a moment. Jenny lay gleaming beside me, not moving, her second skin unscathed by the tunnel walls. There appeared to be no change in her—or was there? When I ran my hand across the surface of her body white threads came off in my hand. What did that mean? I put my ear to her chest.

Was her heartbeat quicker than it had been?

I struggled on. The tunnel slope eased a little, but I was so tired that I couldn't speed up. Above me, and under me, and to the side, wherever the Unearthers were, they headed towards the surface, hoping to cut me off. They no longer bothered hiding their thoughts. They were now purely intent on hunting me down. Every thought they had, when they weren't discussing which way to go, was aimed at scaring me.

Under us Tanni backtracked, wondering where he had gone wrong.

Then—at precisely the same moment—all the Unearthers stopped.

They were listening for me. Listening for a grunt or a heavy breath or careless footfall. Any vibrations I made through the tunnel walls in this silent place were bound to give me away.

So I stopped as well. I hung there on one foot and two fingers. It was torture because my fingernails were bleeding. I shut my eyes against the pain. Eventually the Unearthers moved on, heading back to the intersection point.

Thomas, exhausted himself, was hitting out at Parminder, trying to distract her. She wanted to dump him, but Tanni knew I was listening in and told me this:

"I'll kill him. Are you listening, Helen? I'll kill Thomas unless you give in."

Would he? No, I thought. Thomas's beauty was too important. And even if Tanni meant it, I'd never give Jenny up now.

I forced my body on a couple more feet—and became aware of light. Not the dull bronze of the Unearthers, not daylight even; silver light.

Heaving myself towards it, I heard a metallic scrape and realized that Tanni and Parminder were directly below me. They closed in swiftly. As soon as they were near enough to see my legs they both began screaming, trying to break my concentration and make me fall. In the adjacent tunnels, overhead and already on the surface, the rest of the Unearthers were gathering.

EIGHTEEN

dead or alive

THOMAS

I punched out at Parminder. Just once I wanted to find a way to hurt that disgusting metal face—or at least slow her down.

"Leave Thomas behind," she said to Tanni. "He's delaying us!"

But Tanni said no, and then they both concentrated, their efficient drill-parts propelling them up the tunnel walls towards Helen. So far I'd only caught a hint of her legs lit by silver light. Then I saw the shape of Jenny hanging translucently under her chest.

"I knew we should have killed her!" Parminder snarled.

One of Jenny's rigid knees struck the tunnel wall, and a thin layer scraped from her body. Her arm brushed up against Helen—and part of whatever she was wrapped in flaked off.

"Something's happening," Parminder said.

"Don't talk," Tanni hissed. "Focus on climbing. There's

still time to stop it."

I gazed up. At first only single snowlike puffs of Jenny's skin-covering fell away as she accidentally scraped the walls. But soon whole bright-lit flurries were spinning past my face. Then, as if a hundred birds had shed their feathers at once, a great drift of whiteness flowed down the tunnel.

Helen reached the surface, clambering with Jenny over the rim of the entrance-hole. The Unearthers followed close behind, but when Tanni reached the top he hesitated, and I saw why: Milo was there. Incredibly close to us, his huge eyes stared menacingly down at the Unearthers.

Then, when I looked more closely, my hope faded, because he was obviously under attack. Milo's whole body shuddered. A force beyond his wings was hurling into him. From the booms and shuddering concussions, I knew it had to be the Roar.

"Good," Tanni said. "Their silver child can't move. If he does, the Roar will make him pay a terrible price. He can't stop us. And that means nothing can."

He, Parminder, and six more pairs of Unearthers fanned out from the tunnel, advancing on Helen in a steady line. She hadn't managed to get far. She stumbled along as best she could, pulling Jenny across the mud.

Tanni bent to examine the ground ahead. A thickening trail of white was falling away from Jenny.

"The girl's in the cocoon!" Parminder said, raising her

voice so all the Unearthers heard. "Dead or alive, cut her out!"

I willed Helen to move faster, but she just couldn't. Where she'd found the strength to manhandle Jenny up that tunnel I had no idea, but she didn't have the muscled arms of the Unearthers to help her drag Jenny across the mud. She tried, though. She continued to haul the weight of Jenny southwards and, as I looked that way, for a moment there seemed to be some empty space. Then twenty more of the biggest Unearthers scrambled out from nearby holes. Another group emerged in the east, angling to cut Helen off. Their heavy bodies weren't nimble over surface ground, but they didn't need to be to catch Helen.

On her knees, Helen pulled Jenny south. Systematically, the Unearthers closed the gap on her.

I gazed around for help. Anywhere else in Coldharbour would have been packed with children to call upon, but no one could sleep through the endless noise of drilling here, so this territory had been left entirely to the Unearthers.

And then, in the distance, I couldn't believe what I saw. Walter.

Large numbers of children were with him, and I could just make out the twins on his shoulders. Walter was maintaining an easy pace they could all handle, but when he saw the Unearthers he put the twins down and ran at full speed towards Helen.

Tanni deployed the drill-teams.

"A circular defense formation around both girls," he ordered. "Five rows deep. Don't let the giant near them."

"We can't take him on and all the other children as well," Parminder argued.

"I don't think we'll have to."

At Tanni's signal all the Unearthers lowered their drill-hands, hammering them into the earth. It was a brief demonstration of power, but enough—enough to make it obvious to Walter that even with only a small amount of my beauty to power the drills ordinary children stood no chance.

Walter hesitated, then ran back to the column of children behind. Helen's dad was with the twins. Walter spoke urgently with all three of them. I was too far away to hear what was being said, but it was clearly an argument. The twins slapped Walter angrily, but he was unmoved by their words, though he stroked their faces. Both twins tugged harshly at his jacket, while Walter pushed them mildly back. Then he turned to face all the other children, calling out instructions.

"I thought so," Tanni said. "A soft touch. Walter won't allow the rest to get involved. He's going to take us on alone."

"How strong is he?" Parminder asked.

"It doesn't matter. He's flesh, not metal."

"He might use the bodies of the other children as shields against our drills."

"He won't," Tanni said. "He'll sacrifice himself first."

I stared at Tanni. I only had a meager sum of beauty left in me, and I was determined the Unearthers wouldn't get any, but I was too weak to prevent it from reaching them altogether. Despite my efforts, tiny amounts leaked into them, just enough beauty to turn their drills.

Tanni leaned towards me. "Why do you think I brought you along, Thomas?" he whispered. "Every little bit strengthens us. I knew you'd give in when it mattered most."

"The cocoon!" Parminder shrieked.

All our eyes were drawn to it. Helen sat on the ground, cradling Jenny's head, and we all saw this: the skin shudder.

Jenny moved. Another movement. Another—this one from a limb, like a kick, or a jab from a hand.

Was that little girl punching her way out?

Helen clawed furiously at the membrane of the cocoon.

Walter approached the Unearthers: not rashly; a measured stride taking in the strength of their defense. He stopped when he was a stone's throw away.

"G-get away from Jenny!"

There was deadly purpose in his voice. I'd never heard Walter sound like this, and even through her metal skin I had the pleasure of feeling a shudder from Parminder.

Tanni immediately sent three pairs of Unearthers against him.

The first pair tried a rush attack. Walter waited for them. When they arrived he simply booted their feet away, knocking them across the ground with an effortless flick of his hand. Seeing the ease with which they were dispatched, the rest of Unearthers glanced anxiously at Tanni.

The next two pairs came at Walter together from different directions, front and rear. Walter pivoted to meet the first pair, but while he deflected their attack the second pair managed to press their drills into him.

The drills erupted into life—and Walter backed off.

There was a gash in his leg. Walter examined it, but if he felt any pain he didn't show it to the Unearthers. The pairs attacking withdrew, their drills switching off automatically. Walter stood there, bleeding from the shin.

"So, the giant can be hurt easily enough," Parminder said.

"No, you weren't watching," Tanni replied. "That wound of his isn't deep. He could have avoided the injury. I think he only did it to be prepared."

"Prepared for what?"

"The pain of the drills. He wanted to know what it would feel like when more of us attack." Tanni studied Walter. "He could have killed those I sent. He only needed to use his hands. He chose not to, that's all."

"How do we fight him, then?"

"He'll want to pick us off in small groups. On his own terms. So we'll bring him onto us where our numbers are thickest. Attack the prisoners!" he shouted. "Drill into the cocoon!"

Helen screamed—and with that Walter leapt at the Unearthers.

The speed with which he moved caught them completely by surprise. Most of the Unearthers did not have time to raise their drill-arms to defend themselves. Walter smashed into them, the weight and force of his assault driving them back. But he could not quite reach Helen and Jenny, and now he was in peril, for he was in the middle of the Unearthers. For a moment it was almost quiet; then the Unearthers, leaning against Walter's body, activated their drill-hands.

He stifled a scream, but we all heard it.

The twins and all the other children immediately surged forward, trying to reach him. But they couldn't; Tanni had deliberately placed the largest Unearthers on the outside of the circle. These now touched their drills to the ground, forming an impenetrable ring of grinding steel. There was no way to break the defense.

Walter was alone.

I held onto my beauty. I could at least do that for Walter. I clenched my teeth and gave the attacking Unearther drill-hands almost no power.

Even so, they still had the sharp blades to press against him. To reach Helen, Walter had to wade into the center, where the Unearthers' numbers were greatest. Every step he took their drills entered him. He pushed forward.

"Walts!" came Emily's voice, begging him not to, but he ignored her. I watched him, and I realized that, even at this point, Walter could have got away. He could have escaped. He could have jumped out of the circle and saved himself.

Instead, he pressed on into the Unearthers. Closer and closer to Helen he came, and at one point I thought he might reach her. Battling his way, pitching and throwing himself at the Unearthers, he willed his way through, and had they been ordinary children the Unearthers could never have withstood his assault. But Carnac held their minds and forced them to fight through any amount of pain, and gradually, as they pounded into him with all their combined weight, Walter's arms came more wearily away from them. There came a point when he stopped moving altogether.

Then I heard a cry of rage that shook us all, and Walter's arms plowed forward again. But no matter how many Unearthers he dispatched there was always another to take the place of those he hurled aside, and another, and another, and another.

And then Walter, more wound than boy, raised his head, stared out of the blood of his eyes, and thundered: "Thomas!"

And my beauty responded. From a need this great, not even Carnac could hold it back. The little beauty I had left sought Walter out.

At first—nothing. Then, from the Unearthers piled on

top of him, Walter's back slowly rose up. Yanking out the drills embedded in his legs, he stood gradually upright and bellowed, "H-Helen!" He reached out, and this time her fingers found him. Gathering her and Jenny against him, Walter broke free of the Unearthers—and jumped clear of the circle.

A huge swelling cheer started up as children saw Walter escape. He tottered across the ground and the twins scuttled over to stand in front of him. Walter swayed there, surrounded by children, blood on him, my beauty flowing through him, facing the drills of the Unearthers.

"Get back!" I shouted. "Get further away! Get back!"

Walter didn't understand. He didn't realize that my beauty was ebbing. I'd given him enough to break free, but I had nothing more to give.

Walter tried to rise, then realized he couldn't. In desperation, he stared at me. "Thomas?"

Seeing his opportunity, Tanni ordered the Unearthers to direct their drills at the nearest group of children. "I'll kill them all!" he yelled at Walter. "You know I'll do it! I will! Leave Jenny to me and I'll spare them."

Above us, the Roar had redoubled its attack on Milo. The sound was so deafening that several children put their hands over their ears.

In Walter's arms Jenny writhed.

A kick. A swell. A movement of her face.

"She's trying to get out," Parminder said. "Kill her!" She reached towards Walter, but the twins stood in front of him, and Helen's dad was beside them.

"Don't give 'er up!" Freda shrieked at Walter.

The cocoon continued to stretch.

Twenty pairs of Unearthers jumped over the twins and Helen's dad and knocked Walter to the ground. He tried to get up, to leap away, but with so many holding him down and without more of my beauty he didn't have the strength. He stared disbelievingly at Jenny. He tried again to rise; failed.

"Finish it!" Parminder screamed at Tanni. "Kill the girl. Nothing can stop us now. What are you waiting for?"

Tanni stood over Jenny. The knifelike serrations of his free drill-hand were suspended over her head. All he had to do was press, but he didn't. I sensed a change in him: a shred of resistance, a tiny defiance.

"What's wrong with you?" Parminder shrieked. She brought their joined drills down, forcing Tanni's with hers until the edges were touching the cocoon over Jenny's face.

And then Helen, who until now had said nothing at all, whispered to me: "Thomas, help her. Jenny can't get out without you. Please. You must give her the rest of your beauty."

Helen was crying when she said it, because I think she knew. She knew that the only beauty I had left was the tiny portion keeping me alive.

I hesitated. I couldn't help that.

Then I gave it to Jenny.

A small crack appeared in the membrane over her face. It enlarged, split into four more, followed by a cry from inside.

Then an extraordinary burst of energy knocked all of us back.

I landed some distance away, and afterwards I could barely move. The world around me seemed to be darkening. No, it wasn't that. *My* world was darkening. I was dying. I wasn't going to live long enough to see what came out of that cocoon.

But I had to. I fought against my closing eyes and held back the final few heartbeats I had left, and turned towards her.

The crack in the cocoon widened. Hurry, I thought. It cracked again, split in several places, but whatever was about to emerge did not find it easy.

It was a hard, a terrible rebirth.

And then Jenny emerged.

I don't know what I expected to see struggle out of that cocoon. In those last seconds I just longed for it to come out quickly, so that I'd have time to see it. I glanced up at Milo, and thought that after all Jenny might be like him, a second silver child ready to lift daunting wings and take her place beside her brother.

But she was not a silver child. What reached out from the cocoon was a simple human hand. It was Jenny's hand.

No, I thought. It can't have been for nothing. It can't have!

Jenny's small pale fingers reached around the shell to tentatively pull herself out. And when she did it was Jenny. It was the same Jenny we all knew. "Thomas," she said. "Thomas." She blinked at me, pulling paste off her lips.

My eyes closed. I couldn't open them again, though I tried. I'll die now, I thought. But even in the few final seconds left to me there was no peace, because I felt the full fury of Carnac reach out. He was clutching for me, trying for any beauty he could still rip from my dying body to power his Unearthers. You'll not have it, I said to myself, not even believing I could hold out any longer, just saying the words. I almost smiled, because there was nothing left for Carnac anyway. And even if there had been, I wouldn't have given it up. I'd withheld my beauty for this long. I could hold on a little more.

You'll never get it from me now, I thought.

"Help him," said Helen. "Help him."

I couldn't see her.

"I will," said another voice.

I felt a hand reaching out to mine. From its small-fingered touch I knew it was Jenny. The hand was warm, and that warmth entered me. It was a modest amount of beauty, enough to hold me at the brink of life and open my eyes.

I gazed up at Jenny.

And that's when I saw the fire.

NINETEEN

the wind and the sun

HELEN

Not fire. Thomas was mistaken about that. It was light.

And with it came screams.

The Unearthers opened their mouths, but the screams weren't theirs. They were Carnac's. I felt him in the core of the world, seizing his own jaw in fear.

Walter staggered up on his feet. Gathering the twins in one bloodied arm, he reached out for me, then gently lifted Thomas from the mud. But as he went to pick up Jenny, I said to him, "No. Leave her alone."

"But she's hurt," he protested. "She's—"

"On fire," Thomas whispered. "Helen, she's on fire!"

"It's not fire," I told him. "Don't you recognize your own beauty? It was never meant for the Unearthers."

Jenny was taking everything back—every scrap of beauty the Unearthers had stolen from Thomas. She didn't remove it slowly. She tore it from their bronzed faces. And as it entered her she began to glow. The glow was like a milky and gradually increasing light that ran across her entire body.

"Thomas, Walter," she murmured, and the beauty reached out to repair their bodies. But there was far more beauty entering Jenny than was needed for that. It flowed around her legs and shoulders. It flickered over her throat. It entered her face and riddled her hair with light.

The Unearthers tried to stop it. As the beauty left them, they clutched at it ineffectually with their drill-hands. But nothing could hold the beauty back from Jenny now.

Dad found his way across to me. "What's happening, Helen?"

"It's too much," Thomas said, as Jenny brightened and brightened. "She can't take all of it. There's too much beauty for one person. Even Milo never had so much inside him. We've got to stop this!"

Jenny had not been frightened until now, but hearing Thomas she suddenly was. She started fighting the beauty. It swept over her face, and when it tried to get inside her lips she resisted it, clamping her mouth shut. "Walter!" she cried.

But as he went towards her, a voice above us called out: "STAY BACK. LET THE BEAUTY GO. JENNY, IT IS NOT MEANT FOR YOU TO HOLD ON TO. LET IT GO."

Jenny stared up into her brother's silver eyes. She didn't understand. She thought that perhaps she was meant to be the second defender to hover alongside him in the clouds. She raised her hands, expecting him to lower his wings and gather her up. But Milo shook his head.

"REACH OUT TO THEM," he said. "MAKE THEM COME TO YOU."

He drew in his breath to encourage her, and on the updraft of air Jenny at last seemed to understand. She turned in all directions. She closed her eyes, taking in the vast extents of the world. She sent out a signal.

"What was that?" Freda whispered, as it brushed past her.

Carnac knew. Too late, he tried to reanimate the Unearthers in an attempt to stop Jenny. But the Unearthers did not move; his hold on them was gone forever. Realizing that, under us, Carnac shrieked and shrieked. He couldn't bear to see this.

In those initial seconds after Jenny released her signal even Thomas didn't understand how she was using his beauty. He gazed at the children of Coldharbour, expecting to see a change there. But Jenny's signal had nothing to do with us children. It had a wider purpose than that, a greater one.

It was an outcry. It was an insistent summons. A warning.

And, at exactly the same moment, all the nonhuman life on the Earth heard it—and simply stopped. The entirety of the world's animals stopped. They stopped whatever they were doing, and turned towards Jenny. On mountain slopes lions looked up from their kills. In deserts, creatures forgot the sun. Wolves in every wilderness howled.

"Helen?" Freda looked at me for an explanation; they all did.

I let my mind take in the world. Creatures everywhere were heading towards Coldharbour. In tropical skies, birds were in flight. Bees, responding to their restless queens, had abandoned their hives. Whales of all species were leaving the ocean places they thought were safe, realizing that only one place was safe now.

"Look!" Emily said, pointing skyward.

Black-backed gulls were overhead. It was the ragged remnants of the flocks of Coldharbour. They flew curiously around Jenny, and soon they were joined by individual kittiwakes, terns, and other birds who made a home on the borders of Coldharbour.

Then the first of the insect swarms arrived.

A vast number, flies and moths—all the species trapped within the span of Milo's shield—began to gather over Jenny. There were so many that where she stood they half-darkened even the Milo-made sky, and for a moment we were all afraid they would descend on us. But the swarm stayed in the air, wheeled once or twice around Milo's feet, and then took up a position at the rim of his right wing.

Thomas shook his head. "But why?"

"Don't you understand?" I said. "When the Roar

arrives, the only chance of safety is Coldharbour. We're not the only things on Earth threatened by it. All life is."

"You mean Jenny's bringing *everything* here, to protect them?"

"Everything that can move. But that's not the only reason, Thomas."

"Oh?"

"Do you think only children can defend the Earth?"

I looked over at Jenny. She had moved further away from us, and stood rooted to the ground, a column of light and something more enticing, drawing all the creatures of the world towards us. I was afraid and awed, thinking about the numbers coming.

You resourceful girl, I thought. How are you going to control them all?

Then I felt a change. Jenny continued to bring the animals towards Coldharbour, but some of the beauty inside her was diverted to another purpose. I smiled when I realized what it was.

A different kind of beauty was spreading throughout Coldharbour. And this time Jenny *was* seeking out children. But not all children. Only a selection; only every fourth or fifth child. The beauty brushed against the twins—then bypassed them, realizing they did not need it—and moved on instead to a boy wearing a mud-smeared vest. As the beauty selected him he jumped in surprise, not yet understanding what was happening.

But I knew, and the twins could guess.

"The second generation," Emily murmured. "Oh, Helen." There were tears in her eyes. The boy beside her was mesmerized by those tears. Another child, a girl this time, sniffed the air's moistness. Then, at the same moment, all of the children selected by the beauty—thousands upon thousands of children—suddenly turned southwards.

"TO THE OCEAN," Milo boomed. "TO THE OCEAN."

The chosen were on the move even before his words ended. To the sea they ran, older kids picking up smaller ones. Within minutes those closest to the beaches were already wading out into the water. Rushing to join them, others strained their ears for any sound of waves.

As the twins made us hurry, Dad struggled to keep up.

"What is everyone doing?" he demanded.

"Don't yer know yet?" Freda said, laughing, and running between his legs. "There are enough now. With Thomas's beauty we can do it. We can free the Protector at last!"

Walter carried me and the twins most of the distance, but as we neared the sea Emily saw a problem.

"If I'd a way," she said, twisting her face to peer at Milo, "I'd let it flow."

"If I'd a way, I'd let it go," Emily added. "Won't you?" she called up to him. "Won't you open a wing for uz? How can we find the Protector if you won't?"

"He can't," Thomas said. "If Milo moves his wing the

Roar's bound to attack again."

"Is it?" I said, grinning. "Haven't you noticed something?"

With all the shouts of excitement and scraping of running feet, hardly anyone had heard yet: the drumming of rain overhead had ended. And in that moment I wished every child and adult in the world knew what I did. Because Carnac was in misery. He was in torment and, sensing that, the Roar was truly shocked. She was stunned by what we had done. For the first time in her long journey she had slowed down, hesitating. She had even ceased her attack on Milo, doubting herself.

Fear. There was real fear in her mind, and this time it was not only fear of the Protector.

It was fear of us.

Overhead Milo sensed it, too. He was not confident—what he felt was far less certain than that—but he felt confident enough at least to briefly raise his wings. He lifted them and then flew up in sweeping arcs over us, not high, not as high as he had been before, but far enough so that the children chosen for the ocean could at least feel the wind and the sun one more time before they started on their journey.

Only Walter was still unsure.

"Are you s-strong enough?" he asked the twins, still needing to be convinced.

"We are!" Freda shouted.

"Oh, I wish you could come with us, Walts!" Emily

said, rubbing his face. "I wish you could come down and be with uz when we free it. After all you've done, it ain't fair."

"If there was a way, we'd take you there," Freda added.

Walter held them both. "It d-doesn't matter," he said. "I'll w-wait. Because this time you're c-coming back, aren't y-you?"

"Yes." Both girls hugged him.

On the beaches and in the water there were thousands of children.

"They're waiting," I told the twins.

"Who for?" Emily asked.

"They need to know the way," I said, smiling. "How could they go without you?"

When we finally reached the shore, Emily slipped from Walter's back and looked out to sea. "So," she said, breathing unevenly.

"Can yer hear it?" Freda whispered.

And we could. All of us could. From way below us, not even from this ocean, but another, we at last heard it— the voice of the Protector. It was reaching out, calling to us, and suddenly I longed for nothing more than to be diving with these children.

The twins kissed each of us, their kisses lingering over Walter.

He searched Emily's face for any tell-tale signs of anxiousness.

"I'm ready," she said. She drew her hands across his

cheeks, and kissed him again. "Walts, this time I really am."

Without fear she glanced at Freda, took her hand and both girls swam out into the shallows to join those waiting. For a moment all the ocean-bound children turned back to us and raised their arms, a silent salute to those left behind.

Then, led by Emily, they slid beneath the surf.

For a while Dad, Thomas, and I stood beside Walter, staring out to sea. Above us, one of Milo's eyes was turned back to the heavens. His other eye was reflected as a silver oval in the outgoing tide. That eye counted children. Milo counted the children under the sea. He counted those in Coldharbour. And he counted and saw clearly the other billions still making their way towards Coldharbour. All those children, I thought. Children mingling with birds and every other kind of creature, all on paths they had never taken before. All trying to get to Coldharbour before the Roar.

I stared around me. Most of the children nearest us were looking enviously at the sea, wishing they had been selected to go with the twins.

"So many left behind," Dad said.

"No," I told him. "It's not that. They're just waiting."

"Waiting for what?"

I had no idea, but I recalled something. I recalled what I'd felt when the first children came into Coldharbour after Milo appeared over us. Summer. That's what I'd felt. I'd felt the door of summer opening. I still didn't know what gifts the remaining children possessed, but I knew they had them. And I sensed that if the Roar gave us enough time we would discover what they were.

Thomas was thinking about something else. He steered Walter away from the beach.

The Unearthers.

Thomas didn't want to talk to them, I realized. He just wanted to be sure about something.

"Their minds are free," I told him. "Carnac can't use them anymore."

"What about their drills?"

"They still have those. Even your beauty couldn't remove them."

Thomas nodded and, as we approached the area where we had left the Unearthers, he leaned down from Walter's shoulder and whispered, "Don't get too close. I just want to look into their eyes—to be certain."

"One wishes to talk," I said. "He's waiting for you. Actually, they all are."

Walter trudged forward, warily approaching the first line of Unearthers.

They were standing up.

They stood there, almost at attention, facing us, the last fragments of Jenny's cocoon blowing around their legs.

And in that moment I understood something. I understood why Thomas had admired Tanni so much. I'd not understood it before, but now I did, because if anyone else had been leading them I realized that the Unearthers would still have been lying in despair in the mud. Tanni wouldn't allow that. He'd made them stand up. He'd got them to brush the dirt off their clothes, and remember who they were, and now they all stood shakily, awaiting the arrival of Thomas.

I looked at Parminder, but she wasn't looking back at us; she couldn't. She didn't dare meet Thomas's gaze. Tanni, however, urging Parminder on gently, walked straight up to him.

For a moment both boys stared at each other.

"What we did to you . . ." Tanni began—but even that was too much for Parminder, and she would have collapsed if she hadn't been joined to Tanni's hand.

"So . . ." he said to Thomas, "so . . . you see what we all feel."

Until that moment Thomas hadn't known what he was going to do when he saw the Unearthers. He had no idea what he'd say either, or even if he had anything to say to them at all. But when he saw the steel of Parminder's free drill-hand trembling, he surprised himself.

"You think I don't remember what you were like before Carnac took control?" he said to her. "You think I don't?"

Parminder still couldn't look at him.

Thomas nodded, glanced down a moment, then indicated the Unearther drills.

"You're stuck with them," he said.

"Good," Tanni replied bluntly. "That's good. I don't want my hands back. Even if you could give them back good as new, Thomas, I wouldn't have them." He approached closer, stopping when Walter held out his long arm. "I don't regret it!" Tanni suddenly burst out, staring at Thomas. "Because if it hadn't happened we would never know. We'd never know how dangerous Carnac is. If he reaches the surface, he'll kill everyone. He'll butcher us all!" Tanni studied his hands in disgust. "Look at these things," he said. "Carnac made a mistake arming us with them, though. We've discussed it together, and we all agree: we're going back down. We're going back to wait for him." His gaze took in all the Unearthers. "Carnac's not waiting for us to dig him out anymore, Thomas. He knows the Roar's nearly here. She's encouraging him up, and Carnac's fighting against the influence of the Protector. He's on his way. He's already left the core. He intends to reach the surface at the same time as the Roar. They'll coordinate their attack from two separate directions. That way Milo won't stand a chance."

Thomas bent down from Walter's shoulder.

"You can't go back there," he said. "Ridiculous. You can't fight against a creature that huge."

"Can't we?" Tanni stared directly at Thomas. "I don't see why not. *You* did."

"No . . ." Thomas replied hoarsely. "I . . . I nearly broke."

"You didn't, though," Tanni murmured. "Over two hundred of us were helping Carnac, and you still didn't. I've no idea how you held out for so long, Thomas. I don't think I'll ever understand how you did that."

Thomas said nothing.

"Unlike you, we won't be on our own," Tanni went on. "We've got each other, and weapons, of a kind. Our drills aren't as powerful as they were when your beauty fueled them, Thomas, but they're better than fingers at least. Better than nails. We'll do what we can with them."

"No," Thomas said. "You're taking on too much. Stay on the surface. At least that way you'll be under Milo's protection."

"But I never wanted that!" Tanni said with sudden passion. "Never! I didn't want Milo to have to protect *me*. I wanted to help *him*. I hate him being alone up there! I only ever wanted to stand alongside him. And if I can't do that, I'll do this."

Parminder still hadn't looked up. "Tanni's right," she said. "We'll do what we can. We'll wait for Carnac. We won't let him come out of the ground without a fight. But we need provisions. Food and water, Thomas. We haven't got your beauty to keep us going now. We're going to get hungry."

"Going to feel thirsty down there in all that heat as well," Tanni said, glancing with difficulty at Thomas. "Thirst. I think you know something about that." A look passed between them that made Thomas drop his gaze.

For the rest of the afternoon as many provisions as the Unearthers could carry were collected and strapped to their backs.

"There's only enough for a few days," I said.

"That'll do," Tanni answered. "The Roar will be here before the supplies run out."

"Are you sure?"

"Carnac thinks so, anyway."

"When will you go down?"

"Now," he said. He addressed all the Unearthers. "It's a long climb, so we'd better get going. I suggest we stick to our drill-team pairings to start with, until we see what it's like for us down there. Bigger teams take the lead."

Thomas stepped up to him.

"What about light? Do your faces still light up?"

Tanni shrugged. "Don't know. It doesn't matter. Our drills were made for these tunnels. We still know the way to the drill-head, with or without light."

The Unearthers positioned themselves over the edge of the holes. From Thomas's memories, I knew how eager each of them had been the first time they'd traveled into them. Now those holes were like black pits. They looked no different to the Unearthers than they did to me or Thomas.

Tanni and Parminder were the last to leave, mainly to give some last-minute reassurance to the final youngsters as they dropped. Tanni hesitated at the lip—Parminder was holding him back. For the first time she turned to look at Thomas.

"I know," Thomas said.

She nodded, tugged at her drill-partner, and they were gone. For a while we could still hear Tanni, his voice urging on the youngsters below him. Then his voice diminished and the holes were silent except for increasingly distant clinks of metal against stone.

I stared around Coldharbour. There were children everywhere. Thousands had left to rescue the Protector, but already countless more, all those who'd been waiting on the outside of Milo's shuttered wings, had taken their spaces. So many happy children. Their minds were glad, hopeful, full of relief to have made it here.

I gazed into their minds, and around me at all the children still unchanged, and there it was again, the door of summer. It was still held back. But I sensed an extraordinary change about to take place in all of us.

"What's that for?" Dad asked, seeing me smile.

"Oh, I don't know," I said. "Lots of things."

I looked at Jenny, still glowing, still working hard to draw every animal in the world towards us, and I had no idea what any of us would do when they all arrived. I looked at Thomas, and sensed his most important role was yet to come. I looked at Walter, and saw that he was the same: he was still Walter; he hadn't changed, and that seemed right as well. Even Dad, without realizing it, now held onto his arm with as much faith and hope as any of

Walter's little visitors had ever done.

For a moment I closed my eyes, and was with the twins under the waves. It was cold, but this time Freda did not have to pull at her terrified sister. Emily herself led the way. She and a few others had started up a tune, their voices carrying long distances in the water, encouraging the more uncertain children swimming behind them.

I thought of the Unearthers, and their grim appointment with Carnac.

I thought about the Barrier, all those parents separated from the children, and wanted to see them united again.

I shook out my hair and glanced southwards, where large clouds were slowly breaking up as they passed overhead. I leaned against Dad, and he smiled, and we both turned to stare at Milo, the sun on his wings and the wind, absent for so long over Coldharbour, carrying across to us the faint sounds of children singing under the sea.

also by cliff mcnish:

SILVER WORLD

BOOK THREE OF
THE SILVER SEQUENCE

ONE

the barrier

THOMAS

"He'll never make it," I said.

It was the usual scene at the Coldharbour Barrier: crowds of young children, all hoping for a glimpse of their parents. Most didn't stand a chance, of course— only the strongest adults were able to force their way to the front of the Barrier.

"There are too many," I warned Helen. "If he tries to get any closer he'll be crushed."

"No, he's nearly pushed his way through."

"Where?"

"Over there, Thomas."

I saw him at last—a big man making his way to the Barrier edge.

The last few steps were the most dangerous. Thousands of other parents were jostling for position. If he slipped he'd probably be trampled to death. With great care, making sure not to shove anyone else down into

Coldharbour's well-trodden mud, he squeezed past two burly men and one frantic-looking mother.

Helen walked up as close to him as she could. She wasn't crying, though she had been on the way here. As soon as he saw her, she manufactured a smile from somewhere and reached out her hands. At the same time, he pressed his palms against the Barrier. For a moment their fingers were so close that they were almost touching.

"Dad . . . " she whispered. . . .